The Admiralty Adventures

Treasure of the High Seas

C. E. Cumming

Copyright © C. E. Cumming 2016

All rights reserved. No part of this publication may be reproduced, distributed or transmitted in any form or by any means, including photocopying, recording, or other electronic or mechanical methods, without the prior written permission of the publisher, except in the case of brief quotations embodied in critical reviews and certain other noncommercial uses permitted by copyright law.

C. E. Cumming asserts the moral right to be identified as the author of this work.

Publisher's Note: This is a work of fiction. Names, characters, places, and incidents are a product of the author's imagination. Locales and public names are sometimes used for atmospheric purposes. Any resemblance to actual people, living or dead, or to businesses, companies, events, institutions, or locales is completely coincidental.

The Admiralty Adventures – Treasure of the High Seas
by C. E. Cumming

Published by Admiralty Publishing
www.admiraltypublishing.com

ISBN: 978-1522726319

For all my family and friends.

Pamela

Enjoy the book!

Love
From

x

20/6/16

One

In the early eighteenth century, great naval ships sailed the seven seas in search of undiscovered countries and new horizons. They crossed uncharted territories and worlds in search of mysterious legends, hidden treasures and new civilizations. However, it was a new threat that was to bring the world's best ships together in battle... pirates!

So important was it to rid the high seas of pirates that Britain sent her navy (which was the world's biggest) and ships from all her colonies, deploying her best admirals with the biggest, fastest and most powerful ships to hunt the pirates down!

THE TRANQUIL WATERS of the Pacific Ocean glisten into the horizon, stretching for miles in all directions as far as the eye can see. The midday sun brings out an array of different shades of blue – from the crystal clear blue sky, to the dark blue of the depths of the ocean.

Below the surface a pod of dolphins and a school of colourful fish playfully swim and race each other. As they near the surface, small ripples cut through the flat calm waters. Seconds later the dolphins and fish quickly disperse, as though spooked by an impending presence. Suddenly, the serene calmness of the water is broken.

The large dark wooden bow of a ship breaks through the water, creating large waves as the water is displaced by its sheer size. The bow is that of a *huge* eighteenth-century sail warship – "a first-rate ship of the line" – which appears graceful and majestic as it speeds with prowess and dominance through the water. The dark hull gives way to lighter wood, which is edged and decorated with gold carvings. With its mammoth size and grand splendour, the ship reveals itself in all its glory as its massive sails flap in the wind upon three huge wooden masts.

It's the *HMS Vanguard* – the flagship of the British fleet.

The *Vanguard* is feared by her seafaring enemies – and rightly so. At over two hundred and fifty feet in length, her three-decked warship structure houses fifty-five gun ports on either side; though closed whilst sailing, they can ultimately unleash her vast and deadly arsenal upon enemies if called into action. A red British Ensign naval flag flies upon her bow jackstaff, with another flying upon the stern.

The *Vanguard* ploughs the high seas in her quest to maintain law and order – one of the reasons she is currently at full speed upon the Pacific. Her orders are given by naval command and the incumbent government and, on occasion, her presence and services are called upon by fellow colonies and allies alike – much like they have been now.

Up ahead in the distance a Jolly Roger skull and crossbones flag flaps in the wind atop the mast of a large black pirate ship, *Black Horizon*. The *Black Horizon* sails ominously towards a stationary stricken ship in a nearby rocky cove. A red British Ensign flag flies upon the stricken ship's jackstaff – it's the British colony ship *HMS Charleston*.

Although being smaller in size than the *Vanguard* and pre-dating her, the *Charleston* is still more than capable of fending off any unwanted attention or enemies with her arsenal and cannons.

The *Charleston* is tilting heavily and has a huge hole in her side, having crashed against nearby protruding rocks whilst caught up in a prior encounter with the *Black Horizon*. The *Black Horizon* menacingly closes in, hunting its prey! The *Charleston's* cannons suddenly come alive, determined to put up one last fight, but her efforts are in vain as her cannonballs wildly miss the *Black Horizon* due to her elevated position upon the rocks and splash into the water, having no effect on their target at all.

Up on the deck of the *Vanguard*, a distinguished, clean-shaven, respectable man in his late thirties wearing a blue uniform, hat and medals stands looking through a metal telescope over the port side. His figure stands out against the wooden surroundings as his jacket blows in the warm Pacific wind. It's Admiral Burrell, the highest ranked naval admiral in the King's fleet.

He lowers his telescope and twists it, transforming it into a metal cane. He had his cane specially commissioned, enabling him to have a telescope and weapon in one rather than carry two separate items around. The cane has come in useful on many seafaring missions – including one where he had to fend off assassins wielding razor-sharp swords and shields. Burrell was outnumbered and surrounded by his assailants; however, their swords and shields were no match for his cane, nor his quick-footed skill.

Several crew members scuttle around the deck as the *Vanguard* nears the *Black Horizon*. Contemplating his next move, Burrell turns to his second in command, Commodore Schaffer, a tall thin man with a slightly nervous disposition wearing a blue frock coat with gold laced buttons and hat. In a distinctive Scottish accent, Burrell announces his intentions.

"On my command, Commodore Schaffer, have the Captain haste forth to port and get alongside those pirates! We're going to put an end to their skullduggery and show them who's in charge of these waters – once and for all!"

"Aye-aye, Admiral," replies Schaffer in his polite English accent as he turns and runs along the deck towards the stern of the ship, weaving in and out of fellow sailors as he does so.

Admiral Wesley Burrell was born in Glasgow, Scotland, and as a young boy he had his sights set on a career on the high seas, following in the footsteps of his father, his hero, who had already carved out a naval career before dying of tuberculosis when Burrell was just ten years old. Making a name for himself, and quickly moving through the ranks of the navy to the rank of Captain, a young Burrell caught the eye of the King, who could see his potential during one of the many British naval campaigns and subsequently bestowed him with the honour and position of Head Admiral of his fleet, following the sudden death of his predecessor. Even at a relatively young age, Burrell took to the position as though it were handmade for him and was soon to make an impact.

The vast size and agility of the *Vanguard* has helped not only her nation to be victorious in battle but also her allies. One such battle was when Burrell was called into action by the King himself to command the *Vanguard* against an attack by the conquistadors and the combined forces of the Spanish and

Portuguese fleets. The bruising battle was known as the Battle of the Empires. With Burrell at the helm and in command of the British fleet, they fought off fierce attacks from enemy ships. However, both sides lost many ships in the bloody seafaring exchanges. The *Vanguard*'s honour and hull remained intact throughout, much to the delight of the King.

In another battle, where Burrell's actions proved victorious, he faced off a rogue merchant ship that had been illegally converted to carry multiple cannons after having been hijacked. Burrell helmed the *Vanguard* and played a deadly game of cat and mouse on the high seas trying to apprehend the hijackers. Again, the *Vanguard*'s agility and speed enabled her to outrun, outgun and outpace her enemies – claiming victory once again.

Steeped in history and honour, and always victorious in battle, never once has the *Vanguard*'s fortitude wavered when called into battle!

As the *Vanguard* makes her way towards the stricken *Charleston*, the *Black Horizon* closes in on her. Suddenly the *Black Horizon*'s cannons come alive as they begin firing, hitting the *Charleston*'s hull several times and causing it to tilt further over as her hull becomes riddled with holes. The ship quickly takes on more water and ignominiously heads towards a watery and unceremonious grave.

The *Vanguard* moves closer. In the distance are several small wooden pinnace lifeboats that are fleeing the sinking *Charleston*. The boats are carrying crew members, sailors hurriedly rowing their oars and putting up the small sails to escape their sinking vessel. A small convoy of pinnaces heads towards rocks and land that appears in the distance.

Aboard the *Black Horizon* a dirty-bearded, dishevelled, eye-patch wearing man dressed in dark clothing stands staring out to sea towards the *Charleston*. It's the head pirate – Captain Morgan.

"Leave them. We've got more important things to do… like finding the treasure!" he bellows in his gravelly West Country voice to the crew. He begins to laugh heartily, and so too does his motley crew, celebrating the fact that they've managed to sink one of the King's ships.

Captain Morgan has a reputation on the high seas. He's feared by many sailors, even by some of his own crew, who keep him onside by giving him rum and telling funny jokes. Throughout his thousands of miles sailing around the world, Morgan has stolen gold, treasure and jewels to fund his lifestyle and has become the envy of many pirates and even members of the aristocracy. In the eyes of many countries throughout the civilized world, he is a man with a bounty on his head – wanted dead or alive.

A number of years ago, when Morgan had just declared himself a captain, he was apprehended and jailed for piracy. However, when a riot broke out in the feeble prison facility in which he was being held, he managed to escape and join up with some of his crew who hadn't yet been caught. Morgan's own ship, the *Sea Dragon,* was destroyed upon his arrest by orders of the local governor. Upon making good their escape, Morgan and his men joined the *Black Horizon*'s crew before quickly staging a mutiny against the Captain and taking over the ship. Since that day, Morgan has proclaimed himself Captain of the *Black Horizon* on many a pirate seafaring adventure.

According to representatives of the King's government, Morgan is a traitor to the crown for his actions against his fellow countrymen and, as such, should be treated like one.

"Now, let's see if we can get our hands on the treasure that I've heard so much about! Full speed towards the horizon, see if we can find ourselves some gold!" bellows Morgan playfully to his crew.

Still unseen and unbeknown to the pirates, behind them and closing in fast is the *Vanguard*!

Screechy – a gaunt, thin, tattooed pirate crew member – runs along the deck, falling into fellow pirates. "Captain Morgan! Captain Morgan!" he screeches in his high-pitched cockney tone.

The pirate laughter slowly descends to a dull snigger as Morgan looks at Screechy, exasperated.

"What is it, Screechy? We're trying to celebrate," he states.

Screechy frantically points towards the imposing and impending *Vanguard*.

"This better be good, Screechy!" shouts Morgan. He casually turns around, unprepared for what he's about to see. He slowly opens his mouth in stunned amazement when he sees the imposing *Vanguard*.

"Fire up the cannons!" he screams.

He frantically grabs a rusty telescope and looks towards the *Vanguard* as it speeds towards them. The pirates run around the deck of the *Black Horizon* aimlessly, having been caught unguarded and unaware, not sure what they should be doing. With the *Vanguard* now broadside with the pirates, it dwarfs their *Black Horizon* ship.

Peering through his telescope, Morgan looks on in awe at the grand stature of the *Vanguard* as it bears down on them.

"It can't be! The *Vanguard*," he mutters under his breath.

Up on the top deck, he sees Burrell waving towards him as suddenly the *Vanguard*'s huge gun ports steadily open – primed, armed and ready for battle!

"No... no!" Morgan shouts.

He quickly adjusts his telescope focus and the glass lens falls out. Looking worried he lowers the telescope, lifts up his eye-patch – revealing a normal eye – and stares ahead intently, knowing that they are unprepared for the attack and that they are ultimately going to be overpowered and outgunned.

"Crumbs... Shiver me timbers!" he shouts then gulps heavily.

"Batten down the hatches, lads!" he screams to his fellow pirates, who pay no attention to him whatsoever.

Morgan always played up on the fact that he wore an eye-patch – his thinking behind it being, it made him look more villainous and scary than he really was. This not only boosted his ego, but it helped him lay claim to being the alpha male pirate on the high seas, and the most wanted of them all. He revelled in his notoriety and so-called fame, lapping up the attention and plaudits from fellow pirates who, more often than not, feared his persona.

Aboard the *Vanguard*, Burrell watches the *Black Horizon*.

"On my command, Commodore, open fire on those pirates!" he instructs Schaffer.

"Aye-aye, Admiral," replies Schaffer.

The *Vanguard* gets within striking distance of its cannons.

"Fire!" shouts Burrell.

The port side of the *Vanguard* lights up with cannon fire as all fifty-five gun ports unleash their demi-cannons and demi-culverins. Cannonballs fly and whizz through the air from the vast forty-two pound cannons towards the *Black Horizon*. The *Vanguard* bombards the pirate ship with its heavy arsenal as they return fire with a couple of their best cannons, without any success. The *Vanguard*'s cannons keep firing, repeatedly hitting the *Black Horizon* and causing small explosions around the ship.

Screechy runs through the lower deck as the *Vanguard*'s cannonballs break through the hull, whizzing over his head – with one even knocking off his hat! The cannonballs explode, igniting the fuses of munitions and gunpowder.

"Captain! Captain!" shouts Screechy.

Suddenly the whole lower deck of the *Black Horizon* explodes.

The *Vanguard* continues her assault on the *Black Horizon* as Morgan and his men quickly make good their escape from their crippled ship and jump overboard, abandoning it, whilst still at the mercy of the *Vanguard*'s cannon assault. Seconds later the *Black Horizon* ignites and explodes in a huge fireball.

The wooden hull and structure are blown to bits by the exploding munitions and debris is sent everywhere – including barrels of rum and beer that come crashing down onto the ocean from a great height, having been thrown into the air due to the power of the explosion.

As the smoke slowly clears there's nothing left of the *Black Horizon*, just floating debris that the crew, including Morgan and Screechy, cling onto. The intimidating *Black Horizon*, which once brought terror and skulduggery to the high seas, is now nothing more than floating wood and metal strewn across the surface of the Pacific.

Burrell untwists his cane and creates the telescope again.

He looks through it, scouring the pirate survivors in the water. He notices Morgan clinging onto the debris. "Well, if it isn't Captain Ignatius Morgan, the feared pirate of the high seas. Alas, his day has come."

"What do you want us to do with the survivors, sir?" asks Schaffer.

"Leave them. Let them soak for a little while – give them a taste of their own medicine for a change! The *HMS Victory* will pick them up shortly – they're only a couple of hours behind us," replies Burrell.

Heading towards the *Vanguard* is a pinnace lifeboat with a few people on board.

"Permission to come aboard!" shouts a sailor.

Burrell fixes his telescope back into a cane then checks his pocket watch as Schaffer looks at him awaiting an answer.

"Permission granted," replies Burrell.

The pinnace comes up alongside the *Vanguard*. Ladders are thrown over the side and lowered for the crew to board.

Moments later, a large near-empty bottle of rum appears over the side, being carried by a stout man in his mid forties who is dressed in a blue admiral uniform similar to that of Burrell's – it's Admiral Vanderbilt, from the *Charleston*.

Vanderbilt staggers slightly as he boards, unsteady on his feet. A sailor in traditional clothing and a Spanish cook wearing an apron and chef's hat named Esteban also climb aboard.

"Thanks for stopping by… but we had 'em pirates," says Vanderbilt in his Southern American accent and sounding slightly inebriated. He hiccups a few times. "It was just a matter of time… and tidal direction," he continues as he brings out a compass to emphasize his point. He struggles to focus on the needle.

"Of course it was, Admiral Vanderbilt. I'm glad you and your men are safe and well," says Burrell.

Vanderbilt quizzically looks over to Burrell, slowly recognizing him. "I know you, don't I? Well, well, well... if it isn't the King's favourite admiral! Of all the ships, in all the world... and I had to end up here!"

"If it's any consolation, I feel the same! You and your men are more than welcome to stay, or you can leave and befriend Morgan and his merry band of thieves as they cling onto what's left of their ship on the off chance that you might get picked up. They who, by the way, would've most likely kidnapped you and your men and held you to ransom had we not arrived when we did! Either way, it's nice to see you again," retorts Burrell in a slightly facetious manner.

Vanderbilt shakes his head and looks at him sternly.

Schaffer watches on slightly awkwardly at Burrell's words but holds out his hand to welcome Vanderbilt.

"Eh, welcome aboard, Admiral. I'm Commodore Schaffer."

Vanderbilt returns the handshake.

"Are you with him?" Vanderbilt asks.

Schaffer nods in acknowledgment. Vanderbilt slowly retracts his hand.

"So I hear you... Nathaniel Vanderbilt, are the new admiral in charge of the King's ships in the colonies of the Americas?" points out Burrell.

"That's correct, Admiral Burrell – or Wesley, as the King calls you! Charlestown, Carolina to be exact. You're not jealous 'cause you were overlooked, are you ...?" he says with a slight hint of spitefulness.

Burrell responds with an *"Are you serious?"* look.

Two

For many years, Vanderbilt has held a grudge against Burrell for taking the Head Admiral position, a position that he thought was rightfully his – although no one else ever thought this. Having worked his way through the naval ranks, albeit slower than Burrell, Vanderbilt always somehow managed to plod along, just managing to get by, usually under the influence of some rum.

Vanderbilt hailed from the city of Savannah in the Southern state of Georgia, in the western hemisphere – a place they once called the New World, now known as America. As a young man he moved from job to job, making very little income, until one day he was entrusted with looking after a small boat in the harbour. He did so and was rewarded aplenty in gold sovereigns for his efforts. To celebrate, he went to the nearest tavern and sampled rum, and from that day on there was no stopping him from indulging in his favourite beverage.

This got him thinking, if he was being rewarded like this for just merely looking after a boat, what would the possibilities be like if he were in charge of his very own boat or even a ship! From that day on, he slowly but surely managed to move forward with a so-called career path – on occasion under the influence of rum – in the hope of obtaining some financial reward or incentive, as well as being able to stock up on a healthy supply of rum. The fact that he had limited knowledge of the sea or seafaring techniques was neither here nor there.

Over the years, many of the people who surrounded Vanderbilt would unwittingly get assigned with the work that he was meant to have undertaken, such as plotting the best sailing course to take to a certain destination or coming up with the best solution to battling pirates, etc. Vanderbilt would always somehow pass the buck but, ultimately, be applauded for his actions and decisions.

It is said, over the course of time, that although Vanderbilt did actually have the ability and aptitude to undertake the work asked of him, he would generally just sit back and be lazy about proceedings. As he was slightly older than some of the incumbent captains and admirals, he felt it was his duty and right to become the Head Admiral of the fleet. The King eventually did bestow him with looking after his fleet in the colonies of the Americas after feeling slightly sorry for him, a decision, at the time, many in the King's circles thought ill-thought out and poorly conceived – although they would never dare mention this directly to His Majesty. Time would tell if the King was correct in his choice of Admiral for the Americas.

"*I* was the one overlooked? Interesting perception. Do you or your men need medical attention?" asks Burrell.

"We're fine! Nothing a good bottle of rum won't fix!"

replies Vanderbilt loudly as he shakes the remains of his rum bottle.

"What about the rest of your crew?" enquires Burrell.

"Don't worry about 'em, they'll make land in no time and sort themselves out… They're resourceful."

"Very well. Commodore, can you see to it that… the Admiral and his men get some food?" instructs Burrell to Schaffer.

"Would you and your men follow me, please?" says Schaffer.

Vanderbilt and his crew follow Schaffer. Not watching where he's going, Vanderbilt trips over a loose cannonball and sends his bottle flying into the air. Esteban springs into action and dives across the deck with almost ninja-like reactions. As Vanderbilt loses his footing, he falls into a sailor who's carrying a large crate. The crate falls onto the deck, with the contents inside smashing with an almighty clatter! Schaffer lets out a gasp in horror.

Esteban lands on the deck, catching Vanderbilt's bottle in his hand – inches from it smashing. Vanderbilt sees him on the deck. "Esteban, what are you doing down there?!" he asks. He notices the bottle of rum in Esteban's hand and looks at it, momentarily intrigued.

"Oh, thank you… I seemed to have lost mine," he tells Esteban, completely oblivious to the fact that it's his bottle. Esteban picks himself up off the deck and shakes his head, puzzled. Vanderbilt takes a small sip from his bottle.

"The King's china!" says a shocked Schaffer.

"No, he's not… He's in France this month!" Vanderbilt retorts, hiccupping.

"That!" shouts Schaffer, pointing to the smashed crate upon the deck, which has broken pieces of specially commissioned china plates and vases inside.

Burrell looks on at the commotion, then puts his hands up to his face in despair and sighs heavily.

"That was the King's china," says a calm-sounding Burrell.

"Well, if it were the King's china, then it's a good thing I found that out, cause I'm going to be telling him that, somehow, you were in possession of it!" says a slightly annoyed, yet smug, Vanderbilt.

"You do that. You might want to also tell His Majesty we picked them up along with his other prized possessions from a pirate ship last month and were taking them back to him so he could put his Ming Dynasty china vases and plates back in their rightful place in the palace!" replies an exasperated Burrell.

"They're irreplaceable!" says a stunned Schaffer.

Vanderbilt stares at Burrell, hiccups, then heads off, seemingly unfazed at what's happened. Schaffer quickly trails behind, keeping a watchful eye out, making sure Vanderbilt doesn't trip over anything else on his way to being fed.

"And people wonder why *he* was overlooked! How does an inept imbecile become an admiral?!" Burrell mutters to himself.

Burrell and Vanderbilt have known each other for a number of years. Although their paths may have only crossed on a handful of occasions, when they have met, Burrell was more often than not given the cold shoulder treatment from Vanderbilt. Vanderbilt still carries a chip on his shoulder, bitter about being sidelined from becoming the King's top admiral.

The warm Pacific wind assists the *Vanguard* in full sail as she gracefully moves towards the horizon. Up ahead, dark storm clouds begin to bubble up in the distance. The dark brewing clouds resemble that of a thunderstorm, nothing uncommon for the Pacific Ocean. The *Vanguard* has sailed through many storms in her illustrious history and has always come out the other side unscathed.

One particular thunderstorm stood out, in which the *Vanguard* was en-route to aid a large cargo ship on the North Atlantic Ocean. The ship had been badly damaged in a storm and was adrift a couple of hundred miles off the coast of New York having lost all its masts and sails. The *Vanguard*, under Burrell's command, was battered by huge waves as she crossed the Atlantic. As the *Vanguard* reached the stricken ship, which by now was rapidly taking on water, the thunder and lightning was striking with a vengeance. Burrell and his men struggled to rescue the ship's crew, but ultimately their perseverance paid off and the entire crew were pulled from the sinking wreck just in time.

As day becomes night, the calm waters of the Pacific Ocean make way for a violent electrical thunderstorm that has unleashed itself on the area. It's almost as though the wrath of God is bombarding the Pacific! Large lightning forks pierce through the night sky. Large sea swells force the *Vanguard* up and down like a seesaw through the rough seas, but the vessel ploughs through the waves, crashing at full speed against them, while masses of water are displaced by her bow. Crew members try to hold the sails in place as the wind shakes them violently.

Lightning strikes the main mast, causing it to snap and collapse onto the deck with crew running for cover, the thunder and wind becoming louder and louder.

As the ship dips up and down, inside the lower deck crew members slide back and forth, accompanied by loose wooden tables and chairs. Admiral Vanderbilt also slides around, merrily humming songs as he clutches his bottle of rum tightly, almost oblivious to what's happening around him.

"The storm's getting worse, Admiral!" shouts Schaffer, running towards Burrell. The howling wind and crashing waves smash against the wooden structure; the thunderous sound is enhanced inside the ship's hull.

Outside on deck the storm continues to hit with ferocity and the crew struggle to hold the sails in place. Suddenly, the other supporting masts and sails are brought down by a fierce lightning strike. This storm is the worst the *Vanguard* has ever sailed through. Having battled many enemies on the high seas, this storm is perhaps her toughest battle yet.

The wind howls and gusts, and the *Vanguard* begins to tilt heavily. Huge waves crash over onto her deck, knocking over some of the crew like skittles.

Seconds later, in the lower deck Burrell, Schaffer, Vanderbilt, Esteban and crew members all begin to tilt – eventually falling over. They all scream as the angle gets steeper and steeper. Loud sounds of crashing waves, breaking wood and smashing glass can be heard!

The fate of the *Vanguard* is sealed – that of a watery grave on the floor of the Pacific Ocean. Her battle against the thunderstorm on the high seas was to be her last.

Three

THE SUN BEATS down on a beautiful tropical desert island in the middle of nowhere. Surrounded by translucent crystal-clear waters, calm waves ripple and wash up against the white golden sand. A gold object, slightly covered in sand, glistens in the sun's rays. It's Burrell's pocket watch – which is still attached to his pocket.

Burrell lies motionless on the sand, along with Schaffer and Esteban, as fragments of the remains of the *Vanguard*'s wooden hull float nearby. They're shipwrecked on the small deserted island, surrounded by picturesque beaches and coconut trees.

A beautiful coloured rainbow lorikeet flies overhead, swooping around the men. It lands on Esteban's soggy, and somewhat now misshaped hat, as Burrell and the others begin to wake up, their faces and clothes soaked in water and covered in sand.

The lorikeet walks over Esteban's hat, pads about, then knocks it off his head. The bird flies away, then lands atop a half open wooden crate of champagne bottles courtesy of the *Vanguard*. It begins pecking one of the shiny magnum labels, then decides to peck the top off one of the bottles. As it pecks away at the cork, the cork pops open, spraying a fountain of expensive champagne everywhere. The lorikeet happily tries to drink it up, playfully trying to consume as much as it can!

Drenched in water and sand, the men begin cleaning themselves up. Burrell looks around the deserted island and notices the lorikeet trying to consume the expensive beverage.

"I think we'll call you Magnum," he says, smiling.

Burrell sees Vanderbilt wandering around in the distance at the other end of the island, soaked in water and covered in sand, still clutching his bottle of rum, as though that were his one prized possession. Burrell sighs, then brings out his cane, which managed to survive the shipwreck, and transforms it into his telescope.

He pans across the beautiful horizon and in the distance spots the rest of his crew. They're dispersed over several small tropical islands, but all seem well, in good spirits and relatively unscathed, considering their violent shipwreck. Some of the crew wave at him when they see him through their own small wooden telescopes. Burrell waves back, acknowledging them. He notices there are several islands, on which crates of food and drink have sporadically shored – this will at least enable his men to keep hydrated in the sweltering heat.

These islands couldn't be further from civilization. Without anyone knowing where Burrell and his men are, and with no means of them letting anyone know, they're on their own – for now. However, within this idyllic setting lies danger. Lurking in the depths of the ocean, just offshore, are a few light-grey coloured dorsal fins that are weaving their way menacingly through the water – sharks!

Unbeknown to Burrell and the others, on the other side

of their small deserted island a small wooden boat appears. It seems to be heading for the island. Anchored away off into the distance sits a medium-sized dark-sailed ship – though it's a mere dot on the warm, opaque horizon. A solo figure dressed in black, oars quickly to make land before riding over the sand and coming to a halt. A pirate jumps out, carrying a sword and musket on his belt. He takes off his hat and shakes his long dark hair, letting it fall freely after having been confined to the constraints of his dirty seafaring hat – but it's a woman! It's none other than Charlotte De Viccenzo, known only as the "Baroness".

She fixes her hair, then puts her hat back on and brings out a small worn treasure map from her pocket. It shows the islands and their layout – more specifically, the island she is now on. On the map, the island is marked with a small red "x". Cautiously, she looks around, as though hunting for something, then starts walking. No sooner has she started walking when she trips over something and falls face first into the sand with a thud. Suddenly, Screechy sits up, covered in sand, and looks around dazed at what's happening!

"What on earth …?!" mumbles the Baroness through a mouthful of sand. "Screechy!" she shouts, recognizing him.

"Baroness?" replies Screechy as sand spits out his mouth.

"What are you doing here?! Are you with Morgan? Don't tell me he's after my treasure?" she says in her soulful English accent.

Screechy shakes his head and sand sprays everywhere.

"And what treasure might that be?" asks Burrell, who appears behind them both.

The Baroness quickly stands up, turns around and places her hand on her sword, ready to deploy it. Burrell, Schaffer and Esteban stand looking bedraggled and soggy. Screechy stands up and shakes himself down, like a dog shaking itself after having come out of water, and sends sand flying everywhere. After doing so, he stares at the Baroness, having been infatuated with her for many years. Her looks, charisma and charm are attractive to Screechy, who pines for her attention like a puppy dog, much to her disinterest.

"Two pirates for the price of one! Except one is wanted for treason against her country for being a traitor to the King," remarks Burrell.

Puzzled, Screechy looks to the Baroness, then back to Burrell confused. "Well, don't look at me! I'm here 'cause *you* blew me ship up!" replies Screechy.

The Baroness looks at Screechy, who flirtatiously blinks his eyelids and smiles at her, showing off his black teeth.

"You're looking lovely today, Baroness. Oh, not that you weren't before, mind. The sand brings out your eyes," Screechy affectionately tells her.

The Baroness rolls her eyes at the unwanted admiration.

Screechy and the Baroness have known each other for several years and have crossed paths on many occasions, and each time is no different than the last – Screechy always tries to get her attention!

Since joining Morgan's crew aboard the *Black Horizon* a number of years back, Screechy came across the Baroness upon the high seas. Being way out of his league didn't stop him vying for her attention at every turn. Their "relationship" was clearly one-sided, but the Baroness did occasionally tease Screechy and wind him up with certain phrases or mannerisms, just enough to give him some light at the end of the tunnel, before quickly shutting the door on any ideas he may have had.

Whilst on the high seas, Screechy never really came across many women, so to see the Baroness – not only a rarity in the form of a female pirate, but a proper Lady at that – well, that was a sight too good to be true.

"Allow me to introduce Charlotte De Viccenzo – otherwise known as the Baroness," Burrell tells Schaffer.

"Well, that's what happens when foolish people let you marry into royalty!" she quickly responds.

Schaffer looks on, annoyed at her remarks. "That's quite enough, ma'am, Lady – pirate! You're not permitted to talk back to His Majesty's Admiral. As a traitor, you're …"

"Oh, do shut up!" the Baroness pointedly tells Schaffer, cutting him off mid-sentence.

Schaffer looks on awkwardly at her, having been abruptly silenced.

The Baroness was known in certain circles for being able to take care of herself, whether it was defending herself in an argument or defending herself in swordplay. Her official title of Baroness enabled her open access to many important people within society's elite, including political figures, the aristocracy and royalty itself, of which she married into – the King's cousin, to be exact, a young, naive baron who was infatuated the moment he saw her win a local fencing tournament.

As a young woman, the Baroness would often sneak into fencing competitions and take on the established older males at their own sport. In doing so, she came to the attention of the young baron, who was there supporting a colleague. Ever since that day, the baron plagued her with gifts and gestures, eventually wearing her down into agreeing to marry him, much to his family's objection, as they felt he should marry someone of similar social standing.

Whilst on "official" duty during a royal state visit to the Palace of Versailles, the French King's brother and an assistant suffered the indignity of being put in their place by the Baroness after they spoke disrespectfully of her upbringing from an impoverished background. Much to the gathering crowd's dismay – including that of the French royal family – the men quickly had their smiles wiped off their faces as the Baroness, furious at their lack of respect towards her, humiliated them in front of everyone in the palace's banquet hall. The young baron then bragged to those who would listen that that fiery woman was his beloved wife. Such outbursts were uncommon in regal surroundings.

However, the Baroness had other ideas and plans. Despite suffering constant snide remarks and being stabbed in the back by those in the baron's circles, the true aim of the Baroness's scheme was slowly being unveiled.

Having watched the baron for a while, and knowing he would be at that particular fencing tournament where they first met, the Baroness got to know him well, gained his confidence and trust, and after marrying him was able to steal confidential state secrets and vital information and sell them to the highest bidder. This information could aid whoever owned it, whether in war or to have a hold over allies or enemies.

The Baroness played the baron for all he was worth, until she was unwittingly discovered by a close attaché to the King himself. After escaping during a mass swordfight against the King's guards, the Baroness was able to make good her escape and joined a nearby pirate ship – after paying off its captain. However, after having made enough money from selling state secrets, she started to like her life on the run so much that she wanted to continue to enjoy her life on the high seas. As a result of her failed capture, she was wanted for treason and for being a traitor to the King – who wanted her head!

Burrell looks towards Screechy quizzically. "Do that again," he tells Screechy.

Screechy looks on bemused.

"Smile," says Burrell.

Screechy smiles and the sunlight emphasizes his rotten teeth.

"That's disgusting. Have you never heard of a toothbrush?" Burrell enquires.

"I had a toofpick once, sir, but I sneezed and swallowed it," replies Screechy.

"Well, perhaps it might be time to acquire a new one …?" suggests Burrell.

Screechy nods in agreement. Living on the high seas and eating poor quality food, usually coated in sugar and salt, along with lots of beer and rum, had taken its toll on Screechy's teeth, as well as the teeth of many other sailors on the high seas.

"Perhaps she's here to rescue us, sir?" says Schaffer sheepishly to Burrell.

"Don't be so naïve, Schaffer. The only reason she's here is because there's something of value to her on this island." Burrell knows her reputation all too well. He notices the Baroness clutching the treasure map.

"Treasure, perhaps?!" Burrell says to Schaffer.

"Well, it's certainly not shipwrecked sailors!" the Baroness retorts pointedly. She looks at Burrell slyly and hides her map. In frustration, she shakes a nearby coconut tree. Coconuts fall out of it and land on Screechy's head. He lets out a high-pitched screech and laugh, whilst small birds momentarily appear and chirp above his head, as he falls onto the sand, slightly concussed.

The Baroness sighs and rolls her eyes at Burrell having noticed the treasure map. Schaffer tries to see the map, but the Baroness keeps it hidden out of view.

"Do you mind?!" she pointedly tells Schaffer, who continues to ogle her hand.

"If that map belongs to the King, then, it's our property now!" he proclaims.

"Is that right?!" replies the Baroness, putting her hand atop her sword once more.

"I... I said *if*!" he retorts, trying to backtrack on his initial assumption. He quickly moves away from her and makes his way towards Burrell.

Screechy picks himself up.

Four

VANDERBILT WATCHES MAGNUM finish drinking the champagne and fly away. Moments later, Magnum lands on top of a large wooden object half-buried in the sand. Vanderbilt sees the object and curiously wanders over towards it.

"What do we have here then?" he mutters to himself.

He reaches it and brushes off sand, revealing a treasure chest. He looks on surprised. It seems a strange and somewhat remote place for a treasure chest.

The Baroness continues to brush the sand off herself as Screechy gulps down coconut juice from one of the cracked-open coconuts. Burrell checks his pocket watch, Schaffer looks through the telescope and Esteban reshapes his squashed hat.

Vanderbilt slowly tries to prize open the treasure chest. However, the metal lock is jammed slightly with rust. He tries harder, using his bottle of rum as leverage. It eventually gives and opens. He slowly raises the lid and gasps quietly, so as not to alert the others. Inside, the chest is full to the brim with gold coins and gold artefacts, which glisten majestically in the sun. In awe, Vanderbilt grabs handfuls of coins.

"Yee-ha, we're rich!" he shouts.

The group look over towards Vanderbilt and see him throwing gold coins into the air like confetti.

Quickly realizing his mistake, he puts the coins back to hide them. However, it's too late.

The Baroness looks on, knowing Vanderbilt has found what she was looking for. She turns to Burrell, who in turn looks at her, knowing that this is the treasure she's after.

Burrell and the Baroness stare at each other. There's a brief awkward silence as they all begin to look at one another.

The Baroness quickly makes a break for it. Suddenly, they all run towards Vanderbilt as fast as their legs can carry them, churning up great plumes of sand as they do so. The Baroness uses her sword handle to push and bump Burrell and Schaffer out of the way.

They reach the treasure chest and are stopped in their tracks, stunned at what they see, as Vanderbilt, oblivious to their arrival, starts to grab handfuls of coins again.

"Wow! What is zat?" asks an inquisitive Screechy.

"Treasure!" squawks a high-pitched Magnum, who's watching the group from an adjacent coconut tree.

"Is that right, Magnum?!" Burrell asks.

"Mystical treasure!" squawks Magnum.

The Baroness smiles at this news, knowing that this is indeed the elusive treasure she has been searching for.

"It must be worth thousands!" claims Vanderbilt.

"Try millions," replies the Baroness.

"Have you ever seen so much?!" says Schaffer, shocked.

Esteban throws coins into the air and some of the others join in.

Burrell turns to the Baroness. "What do you know about this chest? This is the treasure on your map, correct?"

There's an awkward pause whilst Burrell waits for an answer. The Baroness looks closely at the markings on the treasure chest. The sides are covered with a form of ancient writing and drawings, and the chest itself is scuffed and scratched, as though it's well travelled.

"If it's what I think it is, then it dates back hundreds of years, maybe even centuries. No one knows where it came from, or even its origins. There's no official record of it anywhere, and no one's ever claimed it as rightfully theirs," she says.

Burrell looks at her, slightly sceptical at her revelation.

"Until now …!" says the Baroness, smiling.

"So, you're telling me that this amount of gold has never been missed by anyone?" asks Burrell.

"If it has, then no one's ever owned up," she responds.

"I wouldn't believe what she says, sir. It's probably stolen pirate loot!" retorts Schaffer.

"Believe what you want, but I wouldn't have spent the last few months searching for it had it knowingly belonged to some two-bit aristocrat!" replies the Baroness.

"Well, maybe you can answer me this. What's it doing here, on an island in the middle of nowhere?" asks Burrell quizzically.

She looks on, slightly hesitantly, not sure how to answer.

Screechy puts a coin into his mouth and bites it.

"What on earth are you doing?" asks a bemused Schaffer.

Screechy brings the coin back out of his mouth and checks to see if an indent of his tooth has been made. It has.

"Making sure it's real!" replies Screechy.

"Why on earth would you do that?!" responds Schaffer.

"Well, it wouldn't be the first time you crafty lot 'ave planted fake treasure to trap us lot, is it?!" says Screechy.

Schaffer looks on, confused. "What are you talking about? We're in the middle of nowhere on a deserted island. I hardly think it merits a set-up, considering our non-convenient shipwreck! Or, did you bump your head and forget that?"

"What he means, Schaffer, is the 'crafty lot' are us and 'us lot' are them," says Burrell.

"I don't follow, sir," replies Schaffer.

"What Screechy's alluding to is that a few years ago, the King's guards set up an operation to lure rogue pirates with fake treasure in the hope that it would smoke them out. All was going well until one slight flaw occurred. The fake gold paint on the rusty coins started to melt in the summer heat and, unfortunately for the King, the guards' trap ended up making everyone look slightly foolish in their attempts to apprehend the pirates," says Burrell.

"Don't look at me. I never fell for it!" retorts the Baroness smugly.

Schaffer and Burrell watch the Baroness with scepticism, regarding her account of the treasure.

"Fine. If you must know, legend has it that over the years this chest has turned up in different places around the world. The story also goes that a while back, some pirates found the chest next to the possessions of a Dutch explorer named Haas in Africa. Locals told them Haas had been searching for the chest in the regional areas along with his guide. Well, they obviously found it, but no one ever found them – they disappeared," she says.

"Jasper Van Der Haas – the world-renowned explorer. I remember hearing that tale too, a tale conjured up by pirates, probably, to scare off anyone else looking for the treasure so they could rightfully claim it as their own!" says Burrell.

The Baroness looks on, wondering at Burrell's statement. "Make of it what you will, but this treasure is mine, and I'm taking it," she says.

"Not so fast!" shouts Schaffer.

"It's mine, I found it!" shouts Vanderbilt.

The Baroness digs deep into the treasure chest grabbing a handful of coins, as the bright-coloured gold slowly begins to change colour. Looking for answers she studies the coins, as a light begins emanating from the chest, getting brighter and brighter.

A high-pitched noise suddenly starts coming from the chest and the group stop their celebrations. They all gather around the chest. The colours become brighter and the noise becomes louder.

"What is that?!" Schaffer asks.

"Uh-oh!" warns Magnum.

The group look closer into the chest, wondering what's happening, as though being lured in by its hypnotic sound and brightness. Amongst the mass of bright, colourful lights, the gold coins begin sparkling and glistening.

"I have a bad feeling about this!" shouts Burrell over the screeching noise. The group slowly and cautiously begin to edge away from the chest.

"When you said the pirates made up the story about Haas's disappearance... they didn't. It came from the locals, and they didn't make it up! I know because I went to the exact spot where the chest was found – only to find the chest had disappeared too!" shouts the Baroness to Burrell.

"Now you tell me ...!" retorts Burrell.

Suddenly a mass of bright colours shoot out of the treasure chest, almost kaleidoscopic, a loud whoosh accompanying it! The colours fill the whole island in an array of breathtaking, magical beauty.

The bright colours and noise suddenly stop – leaving the island empty and deserted! The group have all vanished!

The treasure chest sits quietly, still full of gold coins and treasure. The lid sways back and forth ominously, then slams itself shut. An eerie silence fills the island as the waves slowly and calmly wash up against the white-golden sands like nothing had happened.

The remaining *Vanguard* crew look on from their respective islands, perplexed at what's just happened to their fellow crew members.

Burrell and the group, along with Magnum, all scream as they fly through a black tunnel – a wormhole vortex! They spin and flip uncontrollably through some kind of weightlessness device. Suddenly a bright light appears and the screaming stops. They've all vanished …

A different world now awaits, one with endless possibilities, as they travel into the realm of The Admiralty Adventures.

Five

ROLLING MOUNTAINOUS HILLS and lush green valleys are visible as far as the eye can see, dense vegetation filling the vast landscape. A long winding river runs along the bottom of the valley plain where the steep grassy hills converge. The valley stretches for miles, with other large valleys visible in the distance.

At the top of one of the hills sits a rocky peak, scattered with boulders and large rocks. An opaque orb slowly begins to materialize in front of a mound of rocks, in mid-air, and the rocks start to become distorted. The orb gets bigger and brighter, obscuring the rocks – a portal!

Suddenly, out of the portal – seemingly out of thin air – appears Esteban! He bounces down onto the rocky peak, wondering where on earth he is!

No sooner had a dazed Esteban tried to take in what's happening, the rest of the group suddenly appear out of the portal, one by one in quick succession, bouncing down the rocks and landing on top of him!

Stunned, they slowly begin to move and pick themselves up. Esteban spots Admiral Vanderbilt's bottle of rum in mid-flight heading straight towards him. He quickly ruffles his chef's hat into a landing pad and the near empty bottle of overproof rum lands on top of it.

Finally Magnum flies through the portal, squawking loudly. He flies above the group dazed and confused, trying to get his bearings. The group collectively look around, bemused at their new picturesque surroundings. The lush green location reminds Admiral Burrell of his youth and the vast scenic rolling Scottish hills as he stares at the landscape in awe of its beauty and vastness.

Following the death of his father, as a young boy during the school holidays Burrell would visit relatives in the Scottish Highlands with his mother. It's a place he holds dear to his heart, in part because his favourite aunt would spoil him with home-cooked soup and cake and his favourite uncle would take him fishing on the nearby family loch. Burrell and his uncle used to spend hours of quality time together on the loch, fishing for trout and salmon. He was a father figure, someone who Burrell looked up to. But, alas, he misses this somewhat peaceful and homely setting, having been away from home and relatives for many years due to his naval duties.

"Where are we?" asks Screechy, stunned.

Burrell turns and looks at the portal. "I have no idea. Your guess is as good as mine."

The others look at one another.

Burrell turns to the Baroness. "What was in that treasure chest?" he asks her.

Vanderbilt picks up his bottle of rum from Esteban's hat and shakes it, sighing at the little amount of rum left. Esteban stands up, turns around and fixes his hat – again. In doing so, something catches his eye in the valley behind them. He stares at something moving in the distance on the lower valley floor. Slowly, his facial expression begins to change to that of fear.

Magnum begins to squawk loudly, then flies underneath Esteban's hat whilst he's reshaping it. The bird cowers inside – hiding from something. Burrell notices this as Esteban hesitantly turns around with a frightened look on his face.

"Vamoose, vamoose, vamoose!" Esteban shouts.

The group look on, wondering what he's saying.

Burrell also notices the thing in the valley making its way towards them at speed. His face too turns to fear as the object gets bigger and bigger, closer and closer.

"I think he means run!" Burrell shouts.

Suddenly emerging from the valley, flying over the hill peak, is a huge pterodactyl dinosaur! The flying reptile screeches and wails as it flies over them. The group are knocked off their feet, blasted by the dinosaur's backdraft. They all lose their footing and stumble down the hill into the valley – thudding, bumping and rolling their way to the bottom. Eventually, they splash into the river below.

"What on earth was that?!" shouts Schaffer after spitting out water.

"A pterodactyl!" replies Burrell.

"A wot?!" asks Screechy.

"One of 'em big winged dinosaur things!" replies Vanderbilt, much to the surprise of the others.

Screechy screams at the top of his lungs as he splashes around in the water, panicking and trying to get out.

"Will you be quiet, before it comes back again!?" says the Baroness, trying to calm Screechy down.

Screechy abruptly stops.

"For you… anyfing," he tells the Baroness and reluctantly forces a nervous smile through his terror.

"We'll wait here for a few minutes, just to make sure it doesn't come back," says Burrell.

"Good idea. I don't really want to be on the menu. I haven't even eaten meeself!" blurts out Screechy.

"Tactful, Screechy, very tactful," says Burrell sarcastically.

"Fank you," replies Screechy, oblivious to Burrell's sarcasm.

The Baroness and Schaffer shake their heads at his naivety. Burrell smiles at Screechy; his infatuation for the Baroness is somewhat endearing, even for a pirate.

Suddenly something large moves underneath them. The group are scooped out the water and start screaming!

The group precariously hang onto the long neck of a huge diplodocus which has lifted them out of the river. The large dinosaur raises its head, causing the group to slide down its long neck, over its huge body and down its whipped tail. Its long tail angles itself onto the grass verge as the group slide off. They land on the grass, again falling into one another.

Screechy begins to scream again and the Baroness quickly puts her hands over his mouth to muffle the sound.

"What did I tell you?" she tells him.

He quickly stops, still looking on panicked – as do the others.

"Sorry," says Screechy.

"We're okay, it won't harm us. It was helping us out of the water," says Burrell.

"How can you be so sure?" asks a nervous Screechy.

"Because we'd be getting hunted down as dinner, otherwise!" retorts Vanderbilt.

The group look on as the huge greyish-green diplodocus lowers its head and munches on some nearby vegetation.

"I believe that's a triceratops," Schaffer states, looking on smugly.

"I think you'll find it's a diplodocus," remarks Vanderbilt.

"Well, you're full of surprises, aren't you?" Burrell says to Vanderbilt.

"Never judge a book by its cover! As a matter of fact, I quite enjoyed reading about dinosaurs when I was younger," says a slightly more sober Vanderbilt. "That's the triceratops over there." He points into the distance.

The group look over at a vast lush valley plain at dozens of dinosaurs roaming freely. Huge green brachiosaurus, diplodocus and three-horned triceratops munch away on the grass and treetops. The group look on in amazement. Esteban lifts up his hat. Cowering underneath, a reluctant Magnum looks out.

"It's okay, you can come out now," Esteban says to Magnum.

Magnum slowly peeks his head out, making sure it's safe. He flies out, hovering over Esteban just in case he has to hide under his hat again.

"Are you thinkin' what I'm thinkin'?" Vanderbilt asks Burrell.

"I don't know… What are you thinking?"

"Probably what you're thinkin'," Vanderbilt replies.

"Well, what am I thinking?" responds Burrell.

Vanderbilt looks at him, slightly confused. "Oh, I can't think straight now! You've confused me! Here I was thinkin' you were meant to be the smart one!" he says, frustrated.

"How you managed to wrangle an admiral position in the King's fleet, I will never know!" says an exasperated Burrell.

"I hate to interrupt a discussion of His Majesty's finest, but whatever you're thinking, you might want to share it with the rest of us, considering we're all stuck here together… wherever that may be!" says the Baroness.

Burrell turns and looks at the Baroness flippantly.

"It's not a female's place, let alone a pirate's, to question senior representatives of the King's fleet!" replies Schaffer.

"Oh, really, Commodore?" says the Baroness.

Before Schaffer can even flinch, the Baroness uses her sword and quickly slices off the top button of his trousers, causing them to fall to the grass. Schaffer gasps in shock at her actions as his white long-johns show.

"Well, I never …!" shouts Schaffer.

Screechy, Esteban and Magnum begin laughing and sniggering. Even Burrell manages a slight smile.

"I know it's not my place, but as a royal, a female and a pirate, I have to question your uniform, Commodore!" the Baroness says sarcastically to Schaffer.

"This is an absolute disgrace!" shouts Schaffer to Burrell, embarrassed. He sheepishly picks up his trousers and ties a makeshift knot to hold them up.

"Did you see that, sir? What's the plan, Admiral, before we're forced to defend ourselves against these insubordinates?!" asks Schaffer.

"I'd like to see you try," says a spirited Baroness.

"Well, somehow we've managed to end up back in the Jurassic period when dinosaurs ruled the world," replies Burrell.

Screechy gasps at this news, then gulps loudly – as does Esteban.

"Whatever was in that treasure chest seems to have sent us back in time, millions of years – before humans were even on earth," says Burrell trying to explain it and take in the situation. "We must've gone through some kind of time travel device," he continues.

Screechy laughs loudly and nervously, momentarily fainting at hearing the news! He quickly picks himself up, trying to act as though nothing happened.

"This can't be happening!" states the Baroness.

"Well, I think we should head back up the hill to see if we can get some answers from that thing we all fell out of," says Vanderbilt, sounding somewhat clear-headed.

"Good idea," replies Esteban.

"Yeah, we don't know how long it'll stay open for… Hopefully we can try and get back home," says Burrell.

The group start walking up the hill towards the peak. Amongst their huge surroundings, they're just tiny dots weaving through the long grass in the vast valley.

Six

UNSEEN BY THE group, at the top of the hill the pterodactyl appears once more. It spots the group and menacingly flies through the valley towards them! The group continue walking, oblivious to the approaching danger, until Vanderbilt looks up and notices it.

"I don't want to panic anyone, but I think we should… run!" shouts Vanderbilt.

He points up towards the looming pterodactyl. They all start running, Esteban hastily grabbing Magnum.

The Baroness notices a small forest not far from them.

"Head for those trees!" she shouts.

They all run towards the small forest on their left as the pterodactyl gets closer… and closer. They manage to outrun it just in time. It squawks and screeches at losing them under the dense forest trees.

Exhausted, the group frantically hide behind rocks and undergrowth and catch their breath. Vanderbilt takes a few gulps of his rum to calm his nerves.

The group watch on as the pterodactyl circles overhead before flying away. Burrell brings out his cane and adapts it into the telescope. He scours the area quickly, making sure it's safe for the time being. Above them, Magnum flies around slightly disorientated.

"We have to get out of here," says the Baroness.

"Easier said than done, ma'am… I mean, pirate," replies Vanderbilt.

"What if we created a diversion?" suggests Schaffer.

The group look curiously at him.

"That might work. Are you volunteering?" asks Burrell.

"Well… well, it was just an idea, sir," replies Schaffer, slightly uncomfortable at suggesting it in the first place. He nervously smiles at Burrell, who's called his bluff.

"I really don't know how much more I can take! I've been flung overboard from an exploding ship, me fellow pirates don't know where I am, I've been sucked into a treasure chest that's spat me out somewhere back in time, I'm being chased by dinosaurs, and now I've got an 'ole in me shirt!" screeches an agitated Screechy!

Fed up with his situation, he picks up a nearby rock and throws it. "I can't take anymore scares. I just want to go home," he says.

The rock hits a large grey object that is obscured slightly by branches and undergrowth. Part of the object slowly begins to move – then open! It's a dinosaur eye!

"Uh-oh!" warns Magnum.

Screechy wanders around aimlessly, heading towards it, oblivious to the danger.

"Baroness, I like you, I've always liked you, I've had my eye on you …" mumbles Screechy to himself.

Suddenly the large object begins to stir and move, rocks begin to fall and branches begin to snap – it's a huge

Tyrannosaurus rex! The group look on shocked and in horror as the large dinosaur begins to rise from its sleepy stupor.

"You've awoken a sleeping giant!" shouts Vanderbilt.

"Oh no, it's a tyrannosaurus!" shouts Burrell.

"What do you mean, 'Oh no, it's a tyrannosaurus!'?" Screechy shouts to Burrell.

Screechy turns around and sees the large dinosaur rise in all its glory. Frightened, he screams at the top of his lungs – as do all the others!

The T-rex's jaw opens wide revealing its razor-sharp teeth as they momentarily shine in the sunlight. It emits a huge roar that bellows throughout the forest. Standing up, it flattens the bushes and undergrowth nearby. Its huge stature terrifies the group. Esteban grabs Magnum as they all run for their lives, back out of the forest!

The T-rex begins running, building up speed in pursuit, its huge claws gripping the ground. It gains on the group as it smashes into bushes and trees.

"Now might be a good time for your diversion!" the Baroness shouts to Schaffer, who ignores her flippant remark.

The group run flat out, avoiding trees and bushes as the T-rex gains on them – obliterating everything in its path!

"Help! Help!" shouts Screechy at the top of his lungs.

Whilst running, the Baroness quickly brings out her musket, turns around and takes aim at a large tree with several large branches. She fires twice! The musket emits smoke as the musket balls whiz through the air. They hit the tree branches, smashing straight through the wood and causing them to snap off and fall onto the pursuing T-rex.

The branches hit the T-rex on the head, momentarily

slowing it down. However, the dinosaur smashes through them easily.

"What's your next trick going to be? Throw it a bone, see if it plays fetch?!" shouts a smug, near out of breath Schaffer.

"Only your bones! Preferably with you still attached to them!" retorts the Baroness.

Up ahead is a formation of large rocks with a gap between them – big enough for a human to squeeze through. Burrell notices this.

"The rocks, head for the rocks. It won't be able to reach us in there!" shouts Burrell to the group.

Still running flat out, the group head towards the rocks as the T-rex closes in on them.

Esteban holds onto his hat as it blows in the wind, and Schaffer holds up his trousers as they begin to fall down.

The group make it to the large rocks and squeeze through the gap quickly in single file, out of reach of the T-rex just as it tries to grab them with its snout through the opening – to no avail. It roars in anger at losing them and continuously tries to snap away at them through the gap. After trying unsuccessfully, it eventually gives up and heads off in the other direction, much to the group's relief.

Sweating and panting, the group collectively gather their thoughts as they move through the gap, which opens up into a cave. The dark cave is dimly lit, the only light source coming from the sunshine that peers in through the entrance.

"That was a little too close for comfort. We should be safe in here for a little while. After all, they do say out of sight, out of mind. Let's hope that equally applies to dinosaurs!" says Burrell.

"Well that's comforting to know!" retorts the Baroness.

"And to think we could've been dinosaur food. Our limbs ripped to bits, our bones snapped like twigs… Now I know what fish feel like when they're plucked out the water – poor mites," states a melancholy Screechy.

"Let's try and remain positive, shall we?" Burrell says, smiling at Screechy.

Screechy smiles back. The rest of the group sit quietly.

"It wasn't the best idea throwing a rock at the dinosaur, now, was it?" says Vanderbilt to Screechy.

"How was I supposed to know that a dinosaur was going to be there?!" says Screechy.

"We're surrounded by them, you idiot! Why wouldn't it have been there? Typical pirate – act first, think later!" snaps Schaffer.

"Look, everyone's a little on edge. Let's just take a few minutes to calm down, shall we?" says Burrell. He walks calmly towards the Baroness. "Now might be the time for some answers," he whispers into her ear.

"What do you want me to say?" says the Baroness. "That we're somewhere in time, in the middle of nowhere, being hunted by God knows how many dinosaurs, and that there doesn't seem to be any rhyme or reason as to how we ended up here, or why we ended up here! Something like that you're looking for?"

"What happened to the explorer Haas? Where did he end up?" asks Burrell.

"I don't know. By all accounts, he was never seen again after he discovered the chest, nor was his guide," the Baroness replies.

"You said earlier on the island that the chest could be hundreds of years old. How do you know this?" asks Burrell.

"Documents and maps place it on different continents

throughout the world, in various decades. The same chest, with the same drawings and markings on it. Everyone who's come into contact with it seems to have disappeared," she replies.

"So we could be talking about hundreds of people, perhaps even thousands?" says Burrell.

"Maybe. No one knows."

"I think I already know the answer to this, but has anyone ever reappeared, back from wherever they were sent to?" asks Burrell.

"Your guess is as good as mine," she says.

"That's what I thought." Burrell sighs as he looks around at the rest of the group. Esteban feeds Magnum some pistachio nuts from his pocket as Vanderbilt sits against the stone wall resting his eyes. Schaffer looks over to Screechy, shaking his head at the disdain he has for pirates, knowing they probably wouldn't be in hiding had he not thrown the rock.

Burrell looks at his pocket watch with concern. "It's been an hour," he tells the group. Cautiously he walks towards the entrance and looks out. Outside, a few small dinosaurs run past the entrance chasing one other, unaware of the group. The T-rex malevolently loiters in the vicinity.

Vanderbilt opens his eyes and yawns, then stares at his bottle of rum, in deep thought. He looks towards the entrance then to the beams of sunlight. Picking up his bottle, Vanderbilt walks towards the entrance with purpose, like a man with a plan!

"Where are you going?" asks Esteban.

"Nowhere. I've just come up with an idea," Vanderbilt replies.

Vanderbilt stops at the entrance as the others watch on, curious at his "idea". Burrell wonders what he's up to.

Vanderbilt places down his bottle near the entrance, directly into the path of the sunlight, which hits off it. The sun's ray is magnified and enhanced by the thick glass of the bottle, which illuminates their dark surroundings with bright rainbow colours.

"Voila!" says an upbeat Vanderbilt.

The group smile at Vanderbilt's simple but effective idea.

"Quite illuminating!" says the Baroness.

"Well, it beats sitting in semi-darkness trying to figure out our next move," say Vanderbilt cheerfully.

"Unfortunately all it's doing is showing us where we'll end up once we become nuffin' more than rotten corpses as we fade away to nuffin' in this 'orrible place!" says a downbeat Screechy.

"Well, that's certainly one way to ruin the mood!" says the Baroness.

Burrell begins to pace the stone floor, hoping to come up with a plan.

Seven

MAGNUM FINISHES EATING a handful of pistachio nuts from Esteban then flaps his wings before quickly cleaning them. Seconds later he's flying around the cave, whistling contently as he does so.

"Must that bird create that incessant whine?" mutters Schaffer to himself as he closes his eyes trying to get some rest. Screechy lies next to him, slouched against the stone wall. Suddenly he screams, waking himself up. The others look up, concerned. Not so much for his wellbeing, but for their own. Any noise could attract unwanted attention from preying dinosaurs.

"Sorry, just had a bad nightmare. I dreamt I was being chased by dinosaurs into a cave," says Screechy sleepily.

"What? You *were* being chased by dinosaurs into a cave, you idiot!" retorts Schaffer, who rolls his eyes.

Screechy sluggishly looks around and rubs his eyes.

Burrell looks at his pocket watch again after noticing the angle of the sun changing. "I don't know why I'm even looking at the watch. Who's to say that time even exists in this place, or even if the sun sets?" says Burrell to the Baroness.

"Well, I'm sure we'll find out soon enough," she replies.

Magnum continues to fly around and notices an opening at the back of the cave, unseen by the others. It is partially highlighted by a stray beam of sunlight from the bottle. He flies down to investigate.

There's a small passageway that cuts through the rock. It's sporadically lit from above by gaps in the rock that allow beams of sunlight to penetrate the darkness. Water trickles out of the sandy-coloured rock walls and from the arched roof. Various minerals also ooze out of the rock.

Magnum flies out the passageway entrance back to the group to alert them of the opening. "Tunnel… back there!" he squawks as he hovers over the group.

Burrell looks on quizzically as he quickly heads towards the rear of the cave along with Vanderbilt and the Baroness. They see the passageway.

"Well, I'll be …" says Vanderbilt in surprise.

"Good work, Magnum!" says Burrell.

"A way home, yee-ha!" shouts Screechy.

"Will you keep your voice down before we end up back on the dinosaur menu again?!" says Schaffer.

"Were we ever off it?" responds Screechy.

The group pick themselves up and slowly walk towards the rear of the cave. Burrell holds out his pocket watch and aims its top gold casing directly into the path of one of the sun's rays bouncing off the bottle. The watch casing catches a strong beam of light and reflects it down into the tunnel. The tunnel looks clear, without any signs of dinosaurs or danger.

"How do we know where it goes?" asks Esteban.

"There's only one way to find out," replies Burrell as he nonchalantly closes the pocket watch. He prepares to lead the group into the tunnel when Vanderbilt pushes his way through to the front.

"I'll lead!" he says.

"Are you sure? I wouldn't want you to leave your bottle behind," replies Burrell.

"Oh, darn it!" says Vanderbilt. He quickly turns around and collects his bottle. As he does so, he looks out the entrance and sees several dinosaurs walking nearby.

Burrell brings out his cane and the Baroness unsheathes her sword. They slowly lead the group into the tunnel. Vanderbilt brings up the rear, nervously looking over his shoulder making sure they're not being followed.

The group walk through the tunnel without any incidents, remaining quiet and on alert – until Screechy screams!

"I thought I saw something move!" he yells, panicked.

"It was probably just your shadow," says Burrell, trying to keep a sense of calm amongst the group.

"Oh, right, yeah, you're probably right," replies Screechy as he looks to the ground in front of him – where everyone's shadows are moving around.

"Screechy, I have to ask, but how on earth did you survive for so long on the high seas?" a curious Burrell asks.

"I don't know, sir. Courage, I think, and definitely me charm. Maybe even me looks."

"Modest and courageous, now there's some rare pirate traits," says Burrell, a little flippantly, as he glances at the smiling Baroness.

The confines of the tunnel give way to a huge cave. The cave is partially illuminated by rays of sunshine that peek in from above. Vanderbilt puts down his bottle and places it into the path of one of the rays. The light bounces off the bottle and shines throughout the cave.

The cave's high roof is sprinkled with fine gems and crystal rocks that sparkle and glisten in the light. Other small stones and minerals also glint in the light, showcasing a plethora of colours.

"Wow! Now that's what I call a rock," says Vanderbilt.

"Heaven's above!" says Schaffer as he studies the rocks.

The group look on surprised at what they have come across. A beautiful waterfall flows from the top of the cave down the rock wall into a blue clear pool of water below, which glistens and magnifies the gems and rocks underneath.

Magnum flies above the group and heads towards the roof of the cave. Looking around, he surveys the area for any threat of dinosaurs – checking gaps in the rock, cracks on the cave roof and even under roots that protrude from large trees above, in case of any lurking danger.

"All clear!" he squawks, as he flies back down to Esteban, who is holding his hand out for him to land on.

Some of the group head towards the waterfall to drink the water and clean their faces. The feeling of fresh water on their skin brings a sigh of relief from some of them as they bathe their faces and rejoice in their brief moment of relaxation. The sound of the waterfall seems almost therapeutic given their predicament. Esteban walks with Magnum over to the waterfall and Magnum sticks his head under the water, taking in small mouthfuls.

The beams of sunlight are occasionally obscured by shadows that appear briefly on the cave's stone floor. Above the group roam a few small dinosaurs that graze and munch on the grass growing on the banks of the waterfall. They seem placid and friendly in comparison to the group's recent encounters.

As the group finish cleaning themselves, they all sit down and relax – albeit for a brief moment.

"Where do you think this will lead us to?" the Baroness asks Burrell.

"Well, we seem to be heading back in the direction we initially came from. So, if we can keep heading this way, then perhaps we might get back to the portal."

"If it's still there," says a slightly despondent Baroness.

"Not the most comprehensive of plans, though, is it? But I suppose it will do given our circumstances. Not everyone can come up with ideas like I did with the bottle," says Vanderbilt.

"Mmmm, and such a gift to have too," retorts Burrell as he stands up to survey the cave again. "Magnum, can you see if there are any more tunnels or passageways coming in here?" He speaks reluctantly, not knowing if Magnum will actually fully understand the instruction.

Magnum squawks in acknowledgment and flies off, momentarily disappearing from view.

"Well, that went better than expected," Burrell mutters to himself.

He takes off his now slightly weathered admiral's jacket and hat and gives them to Schaffer to hold, then rolls up his sleeves slowly and methodically with purpose. "I'll be back in a minute," he tells Schaffer.

"Why? Where are you going, sir?" Schaffer asks.

"Exploring!" he replies with a smile.

"I don't think that's one of your best ideas, sir, given our present situation."

"On the contrary, Schaffer, it's exactly the idea we need right now."

The Baroness looks on impressed at Burrell's gutsy attitude.

Vanderbilt shakes his head, then turns to the Baroness. "See, that's the difference between him and I. That's what happens when you grow up on a small – albeit powerful – island in the middle of the Atlantic: you're bound to want to learn how to climb and be all about exploring! Not I, no. I'm much more of a practical type of gentleman – the older, wiser gentleman, you might say. Yep, that was the type of etiquette I was taught in Georgia," says Vanderbilt.

"For want of a better phrase, some might say lazy …?" retorts the Baroness.

"Well, it depends entirely on what side of the fence you're sittin' on dear."

"Sitting being the operative word on this occasion, wouldn't you say?" she quickly replies.

Climbing opposite them, making his ascent, is Burrell, who's using gaps and cracks in the rock face to get a handgrip and foothold. Esteban and Schaffer watch on concerned as Burrell struggles to reach the top. He brings out his cane and jams it into a tight gap, giving himself some leverage. He pulls himself up, balancing on the cane slightly precariously.

"Are you sure that fing will 'old you?!" shouts Screechy. His voice echoes throughout the cave.

"Screechy!" retorts the Baroness.

"Oh, right, sorry, yeah, I'm not meant to make any noise. Sorry, forgot." He holds his hand up to his mouth.

Burrell manages to balance himself enough to enable him to peer out one of the gaps at the top. Up ahead in the distance he can see the portal glowing at the top of an adjacent hill. He smiles, relieved it's still there. He also notices some thick storm clouds forming. He quickly begins his descent, using his cane as support and leverage, and makes it to the bottom unscathed.

"It might get dark soon, there's some storm clouds brewing." He folds down his sleeves and dusts off loose mud from his shirt before putting his jacket and hat back on.

"We should build a small fire to keep us warm and to ward off any danger," says Burrell.

"Good idea, sir," says Schaffer.

"Did you find anymore tunnels, Magnum?" Burrell asks.

"One! Small – on the other side," squawks Magnum.

"Good. Now that we know what we're dealing with, hopefully we'll be able to contain any outside threat."

Esteban and Schaffer look at Burrell, contemplating his comments.

"We'll just have to be imaginative, given our resources," he says with an upbeat tone and smile.

Eight

DARKNESS SETS IN as thunder claps sound. Magnum flies through the air carrying branches and twigs in his beak as he makes his way towards a small pile of already gathered twigs and branches on the floor. He drops them onto the pile, which is as yet an unformed stack. The rest of the group also collect nearby branches and twigs and take them back to the pile. As little as they are in quantity, collectively they begin to create a larger pile for a fire.

"Make sure you only bring back dry twigs and branches – that way we won't create too much smoke. The last thing we need is unwanted attention!" Burrell warns the group.

Screechy arrives carrying a handful of rounded stones that have smooth carved-out insides.

"Screechy… what happened to the twigs and branches?" Burrell enquires.

"That's a very good point, sir, I can see why you'd ask me that. Well, I fot the group needed some cheerin' up, seein' what's happened. So, I found these and fot I could make everyone some tea," he replies.

"Tea?" asks Burrell, slightly surprised and confused.

"Yes, help calm everyone down. I've got a bag in me pocket that I managed to grab before you blew me ship up, ain't I? It's a bit wet mind," he answers. "We can use a piece of rope from me jacket, tie it somehow to the stones, and then we can hold 'em over the fire and we can all 'ave some hot tea."

"That's... very resourceful and thoughtful of you."

"That's what I fot too," replies Screechy.

"Won't the rope burn though?" Burrell quizzically asks.

"It might, but we've got plenty of it!" Screechy replies, smiling before he heads off towards the group.

Burrell smiles at Screechy's initiative, knowing that this is exactly what the group needs. Schaffer, on the other hand, notices Screechy carrying the rocks. "Typical pirate, never a team player, always mind thyself. Ask them to do one thing and they do another!" he mutters to himself.

Esteban sits next to the accumulated mass of branches and twigs, striking two stones together underneath the pile trying to create a spark. After a few unsuccessful attempts, he eventually strikes a spark big enough to form a small but significant flame. The flame takes hold of one of the branches and slowly ignites, begins to spread and creates the fire. Esteban smiles, as do the others, content at his work.

"Where did you learn to do that?" Vanderbilt asks him.

"At home. My family couldn't afford any fuel for cooking, so I taught myself to create fire to burn on our stove," he replies.

The cave becomes dark as the daylight slowly disappears behind the storm clouds. Loud thunder claps strike nearby, echoing through the cave. Some of the group look on concerned, as Vanderbilt's bottle no longer emits any light. The fire, however, provides enough light to illuminate the main area in which the group are housed.

"Well, that was well timed, but how are we going to protect ourselves from any unwanted intruders?" asks the Baroness to Burrell.

"Make sure your musket is loaded, and keep your sword unfastened in case you have to react quickly. I'll keep my cane at the ready. We just have to hope nothing comes in. Let's hope the thunder scares them away!" he replies.

At that moment Esteban comes to speak with him.

"If I may, I have an idea," he tells them.

"You're quite the cook, Esteban!" Burrell says heartily.

"Thank you, sir. The idea's not much, just an old trick I used to use on pirates: my pistachio nuts. We could lay a handful of them at the entrances. That way if any dinosaurs come in, we'll hear them standing on them," he says.

"Good idea. Why didn't I think of that?" Burrell replies.

"You didn't grow up in a tough Spanish neighbourhood!" Esteban says.

"He has a point!" retorts the Baroness.

"There could be one slight flaw, however. It might work as unintentional bait," replies Burrell.

"This is true, but we don't have many other options," says Esteban.

Burrell momentarily ponders over the idea then nods in agreement.

Esteban leaves them and digs into his apron for his stash of pistachio nuts. He grabs a thick branch from the fire and a handful of nuts and makes his way to the respective entrances putting down enough of them to create a potentially lifesaving warning for them. The flame from the lone branch reflects off the stone walls, brightening up Esteban's path and highlighting the layout and positioning of the pistachio nuts.

Back at the fire, Screechy brings out his one large semi-damp teabag from his pocket and proceeds to rip it open. Burrell watches on curiously at his actions – as does Schaffer. Screechy shakes the teabag over the stones, which now have water in them, and tries his best to give equal amounts of measured tea to the group without spilling any. To do this, he briefly counts the tea leaves before losing count, which results in him resorting to tipping the bag into the respective stones.

"I'm not drinking that," mutters Schaffer.

"Why not?" enquires Burrell.

"It's probably laced with arsenic! You know what these pirates are like, and the ones in our company are no exception."

"A little melodramatic, don't you think?" says Burrell. "As crazy as this may sound, I actually believe 'our' pirates are good people. Sure, they're the enemy, but here we're all the same. There's no them and us, it's all of us together. We have to work as a team now, and a team requires trust. You might have your doubts, as do I, but trust is earned, and they, in my book, have earned our trust."

Burrell walks away, leaving the words to resonate with Schaffer, who sighs slightly at having been spoken to by his superior.

When Esteban rejoins the group, Screechy is already boiling some of the rocks over the fire. They're held in place with makeshift knots made from redundant rope from his jacket. The stones hang from a large branch finely balanced to take the weight.

"Nuffin' like a good ol' knees up with some friends. When I say 'friends', I mean non-enemies, as it were, if you know what I mean?" says Screechy with a slightly nervous smile, knowing that he's still technically an enemy of the crown.

"Touché," responds Burrell.

"I'll drink to that!" remarks a sarcastic Baroness.

Schaffer looks on, still slightly reserved.

"I fink I will too," replies Screechy.

Nine

As the group finish off their tea, Burrell and Schaffer, carrying large lit branches, carry out final checks on the entrances. They see bunches of pistachio nuts sporadically placed near the entrance they arrived in through as well as the entrance into the tighter tunnel at the rear of the cave.

"What happens if a dinosaur comes in and eats the nuts when we're sleeping… what then?" asks Schaffer slightly worried.

"I'm trying to be a little more optimistic than that Schaffer! We need to stay positive… for the sake of the group," replies Burrell, knowing his inadequate answer is of little help.

"Just a thought," Schaffer says.

"Mm …"

They both continue their checks as thunder rumbles in the distance.

"We'll make sure everyone is round the fire place tonight and we'll each take turn at guard duty. I'll go first and then we'll sort out a plan for the others," says Burrell, taking command of the situation.

"Sir, do you think they know we're missing yet… the navy?" asks Schaffer.

"Honestly, I don't know. Apart from the *HMS Victory* being in the Pacific, no other vessels were bound to meet us at our coordinates. As for the rest of the crew… well, they'll be okay for the time being. They have food, water and each other," says Burrell, trying to put a brave face on preceding events.

"Do you think if we use the thing we fell out of… we can get back home?" asks Schaffer.

"That's the plan, but we'll have to wait and see. Come, let's get back to the others."

Burrell and Schaffer head back to the rest of the group, who are finishing off the remnants of their tea.

"I must say, that tea malarkey was quite refreshing. Not quite rum, but it wasn't half bad, Screecher," says Vanderbilt.

"It's Screechy, and, unfortunately, that was all I had. If me ship hadn't been blown up, then I might've had more, but you know, that's life innit?" he replies.

Burrell and Schaffer rejoin the others.

"The entrances look secure for now. We'll each take turn on guard duty. I'll go first," says Burrell.

"When you say guard duty, what exactly do you mean …?" asks Screechy.

"Well, we each take a turn keeping an eye out for anything suspicious when the rest of us are sleeping," says Burrell.

"What, like, you mean the person would be awake the whole time when everyone else is sleeping …? That's a bit scary innit?!" retorts Screechy.

"It's either that or we all try and stay awake… which, given the fact that we're nearly dead on our feet, might not be the best course of action. It's been a very long day and now seemingly night, and we all need some rest," replies Burrell.

"I'll second that!" says Vanderbilt. "We need our rest… give us time to clear our heads."

"Okay, are we all agreed on that? We arrived here as a group, and a group we have to be. So, are we all in agreement?" asks Burrell.

The group collectively nod in agreement as Burrell brings out his pocket watch from his jacket and detaches it from its chain.

"Good. We'll use this for hourly shifts. I'll take the first. Schaffer you're up next, then the Baroness, Esteban, Screechy and Vanderbilt," Burrell tells them.

The group begin to get comfortable for their long, if not slightly nervous night ahead, as Burrell stokes the fire, adding branches to keep the flames alive and burning.

As the group cover themselves with what little clothing they have, Schaffer and Screechy keep their eyes slightly open – their eyeballs scouring back and forth as they keep a watchful eye on things. However, slowly but surely, their eyes become heavier and close from sheer exhaustion.

Burrell quietly paces the area, carrying his cane for protection, keeping a watchful eye out on proceedings. His footsteps echo slightly as they reverberate off the stone walls amongst an eerie silence which has now befallen them. The only constant sound is the waterfall, which somehow provides a therapeutic calm. The silence is occasionally broken by Screechy's light snoring and Vanderbilt's mumbling. Even Magnum is sleeping quietly atop Esteban's hat, which he's using as a pillow. The fire, too, fills the air with intermittent crackles as the branches and twigs burn away, keeping the group safe and warm.

Time slowly passes for Burrell as he watches over the group, who are now sound asleep. Light snoring fills the cave and is momentarily disrupted by a high-pitched squeak. Burrell looks around but can't see anything, until a moving shadow catches his eye – a bat. Above the group are a small colony of bats that seem to have made their home for the evening adjacent to the protruding tree roots. The colony is far enough away from the group not to feel threatened by their presence. Soon the bats, too, quieten down and settle in for the night.

Burrell takes the weight off his feet and sits down near the group, listening for any other unusual activity – nothing sounds. The quietness allows him a moment to pause and reflect on events. Many things go through his mind. He thinks of his stranded crew and their wellbeing upon the Pacific desert islands – will they be rescued? Will they be found? He wonders if the group can ever get home and be with their loved ones again. He slowly closes his eyes.

The sound of a rock falling suddenly startles Burrell awake! He looks around but can't see anything, then looks at his watch. He's been asleep for a few minutes. He forces himself awake. Not wanting to let his group down, he picks himself up, takes a few deep breaths and quietly checks the entrances – all seems well.

Burrell checks his pocket watch. His hour has passed quickly, if uneventfully, which is what he was hoping for. He goes over to Schaffer, who is sound asleep, and shakes him. He doesn't respond. Burrell prods him with his cane. He slowly stirs, still half asleep wondering what's happening.

"What is it, sir? What's happened? Is it pirates?!" asks a somewhat sleepy and confused Schaffer.

"It's time for your shift," says Burrell quietly.

"Oh… what… already?" replies Schaffer, yawning.

"Afraid so, that was the deal."

Schaffer rubs his eyes and yawns heavily as he picks himself up. Burrell hands him his cane and pocket watch.

"In one hour from now, wake the Baroness and make sure she wakes Esteban afterwards and so forth," says Burrell.

"Right, sir, will do," replies Schaffer, sounding more awake and alert.

With night having now fallen, Burrell sits down next to the group and gets himself comfortable for a night's sleep as Schaffer walks to the waterfall and drinks a few handfuls of water, splashing some onto his face to wake himself up. He quickly cleans himself up, takes the cane and prepares himself for guard duty. Trying to put on a tough persona, Schaffer begins walking towards the darker areas of the cave to carry out his checks. However, he quickly changes his mind when he sees how dark it really is and decides to keep to the lit areas instead.

He checks the pocket watch and sighs. Only ten minutes have passed – it seemed longer. Bored, he decides to entertain himself. He brings up the cane and holds it waist height in his palm, as though holding a rifle. He marches, swinging his arm and holding the cane as though in a military regiment, until the cane slips, falls between his legs and trips him up! He falls to the ground, but quickly bounces back up so as not to attract any unwanted attention from the others. He looks over at the group to see if his faux pas was witnessed. It wasn't – they're all sound asleep, much to his relief.

Pretending nothing happened, Schaffer dusts himself down and continues with his guard duty of the cave. As the fire crackles in the quietness, he looks around, slightly nervous at being on his own. As he continues walking, he begins to hear a crunching sound, which sounds nearby and echoes slightly. He slows down and looks around. The sound continues, but has slowed down. Looking around, he becomes slightly scared – it sounds like a pistachio nut is being squashed! He moves quickly towards one of the entrances, trying to work out if it's coming from there. However, in doing so, the crunching sound speeds up. He quickly turns around and looks at the others to see if any of them are awake and hear the noise. They're not – they're all still fast asleep.

Slightly unnerved and looking around cautiously, Schaffer is worried. As the light from the fire begins to diminish towards the entrance, he stumbles on the rocky cave flooring. In doing so, a pistachio nut dislodges itself from the sole of his shoe – which catches his attention. He sighs in relief, hoping that was the noise. He wipes his brow clear of the gathering beads of sweat that have developed, composes himself once again and sets off on his duties, occasionally walking as though he belongs in the King's guard. His time slowly passes – uneventfully.

As Schaffer's hour finally comes to an end, he wakes up the Baroness for her stint. Without question, she takes the watch and the cane and sets about her guard duties. Vanderbilt's light snoring fills the air. Keeping a cautious eye out, the Baroness places one hand near her sword in case she has to react quickly. Slowly and quietly she begins her patrol as Schaffer gets comfy and settles for the night.

The Baroness sits down atop a large rock. Everything

seems quiet. Contemplating her situation, she looks around and wonders almost in bewilderment at what's happened to them. She brings out her treasure map and looks at it. She knew the treasure chest had a reputation and an aura of mystery about it, but in no way did she ever imagine its power or capabilities of transporting people to another place, let alone another time.

She brings out her musket and checks it, making sure the trigger mechanism is working okay and that it's loaded with musket balls. She brings out her sword and inspects it for damage. Both her musket and sword are in fine working order. After putting back her musket and sword, the Baroness walks to the fire and stokes it to create more flames. The wood crackles as small embers float above the fire. The group remain sound asleep.

The Baroness picks up a lit branch and heads off towards the rear entrance. Holding the branch in front of her head, she carries the cane primed and ready for any unwanted guests.

Ten

BURRELL SLOWLY OPENS his eyes. Strong sunlight pierces through the cracks above, illuminating the cave. The fire lies quietly smouldering as remnants of the branches and wood lie in burnt ruins. He looks around and notices all of the group are sound asleep. It takes a few seconds for that image to sink in – that means no one is on guard duty!

He's quickly jolted awake by a screech. The sound is deeper and larger than that of any bat. Pushing himself off the rocky wall, he sees his cane on the ground and quickly picks it up, arming himself. In doing so, he notices remains of pistachio nutshells on the ground and a small trail down Screechy's clothing. What's happened?

"Oh, no," he mumbles to himself as realization kicks in.

The screech sounds again – only this time louder and nearer.

"Get up! Get up!" Burrell shouts at the top of his lungs. The group collectively and slowly wake up, some of them mumbling at the unwanted intrusion.

"Who was meant to be on guard duty…?!" Burrell enquires.

Screechy, Vanderbilt and Esteban look at one another as they wonder, yawning in the process.

"What happened to the pistachio nuts, Screechy?" asks Burrell.

Screechy looks at his top and sees them. "Oh …" he mutters. "Well, sometimes when I'm hungry, I sleepwalk, sir …"

"Now you tell us!" Burrell replies.

"That's not what I think it is, is it?!" asks a slightly agitated Schaffer noticing the nutshells.

"What, breakfast?" enquires Screechy, oblivious to what Schaffer is asking.

"No, you nincompoop! You ate the nuts! They were supposed to keep intruders out – how could you?!" Schaffer slaps Screechy on the chest in anger and dust, dirt and pistachio nutshells fly off.

A loud screech followed by a couple of quieter ones ring out and echo throughout the cave. The group look on slightly apprehensive and worried.

"What was that?" asks the Baroness.

"Get ready to run. I think we might have company!" Burrell informs them.

"Uh-oh," mutters Magnum.

With the group looking on worried, the Baroness brings out her sword. Armed with his cane, Burrell cautiously walks towards the tunnel they arrived in through, tiptoeing quietly. As he nears, noises sound, like claws hitting off stone and dull muffled roars. He peeks his head slowly round the rocky wall… and gasps. He quickly puts his hand up to his mouth to muffle the sound – but it's too late. Removing his hand, he turns to the group and shouts "Run!"

Burrell starts sprinting towards the group with his cane

raised as suddenly behind him, running towards him through the rocky tunnel, appears a menacing pack of three velociraptor dinosaurs charging at him! Without hesitation, Vanderbilt grabs his bottle of rum as the group scream in fear of their lives! They start running towards the rear tunnel as fast as their sleepy legs will carry them.

"Follow me!" shouts Vanderbilt, quickly taking the lead.

"If we get eaten, Screechy, it's your fault!" screams Schaffer in a blind panic.

"How was I supposed to know they were looking for the nuts?!" shouts an agitated Screechy.

"It's *us* they're looking for, you idiot!" shouts Schaffer, exasperated. Screechy screams at the top of his lungs as the realization sinks in – they're back on the menu!

The pack of velociraptors, which resemble small versions of the T-rex, snap their jaws furiously, their razor sharp teeth glistening in the sunlight as they hunt down their human prey.

The group run flat out. The Baroness also now holds her musket in hand, ready to fire. Magnum flies above them, squawking as he too makes good his escape. The dinosaurs gain on them quickly as Vanderbilt leads the group through the tight rear tunnel. Burrell brings up the rear of the group as the dinosaurs snap at his jacket, missing him by millimetres. As the tunnel gets smaller and tighter, in their haste the dinosaurs bunch up too closely together and squash against one another as they each try to squeeze through. The group continue running flat out whilst the velociraptors fight amongst themselves – angry at having lost their prey. However, the clever and cunning dinosaurs have another idea. They quickly double back, head out the main entrance and split up, continuing their hunt another way.

As Vanderbilt leads the group quickly through the tunnel, a light appears in the distance – an opening! The light starts to become brighter as the group fight their way through vines, shrubbery and tree roots. Vanderbilt eventually leads the group out of the tight tunnel onto a rocky hill laced with mist that steadily leads down to a vast plateau at the bottom, seemingly hundreds of yards into the distance.

The group steady themselves as they stand slightly uneasily, given their angle and terrain, as the morning sun tries to penetrate through the mist, casting eerie shadows in its wake. Rocky cliff walls surround the group, as do large overhanging vines, trees and plants with exceptionally large leaves. The mist adds a sense of mystery and eeriness to the location. As Burrell finally exits the tunnel, the group look around, checking for any danger. For the time being, they are safe.

The rocky hill looks as though it's been gorged out over the centuries, as though moulded through the years by torrents of cascading water. The way it cuts through the rocks and undergrowth with such precision and direction seems odd, given the almost jungle-like surroundings and vegetation.

Burrell studies the landscape.

"What are you looking for?" asks the Baroness.

"The portal… I'm trying to get our bearings," he replies, bringing out his telescope and scouring the landscape for higher ground. He peers through the telescope and adjusts the focus, making out the portal in the distance through trees and rocks.

Through the mist, quietly and initially unobserved by the group, the velociraptors make their way through undergrowth near the top of the hill and see the group ahead of them down in the distance. They slowly look at one another, then group together and plan their assault. Magnum spots some bushes moving and sees the dinosaurs lying in wait. He alerts the group. "Uh-oh, dinosaurs!" he shouts as he flaps his wings to get their attention.

The group turn around and see the dinosaurs emerging from the undergrowth. They slowly position themselves in a pincer formation, edging menacingly closer towards them.

Schaffer and Screechy let out a collective scream!

"Guys, you're not helping!" the Baroness tells them.

Burrell quickly transforms his telescope into the cane and takes aim. The Baroness, too, is primed with her musket and sword still in hand.

"This isn't good," says Burrell.

"What do we do now?" the Baroness asks Burrell.

"The portal's up there," he says, pointing over towards a hilly region in the distance. "We have to get to it if we can."

"How?" the Baroness enquires.

Contemplating their predicament, Burrell quickly tries to come up with a plan – as the velociraptors malevolently close in on them and tighten their formation around the group. Burrell ushers the others behind him, for their own protection, and raises his cane in a threatening manner towards the ever-nearing dinosaurs.

"We're doomed!" shouts Screechy.

"Again, not helping, Screechy!" replies the Baroness.

"Sorry, I'm a nervous wreck …!"

"What about the leaves?! We can use them. They look strong enough to hold us," shouts Esteban.

"And do what with them? Throw them at the dinosaurs… hoping they'll eat them instead of us?!" asks an agitated Schaffer.

"No, throw them down the hill… with us on them!" replies Esteban.

"What?! Have you lost your senses?!" shouts Schaffer.

"Great idea… I'll second that, seeing as it's the best and only plan we have!" retorts Vanderbilt.

"Admiral, you can't be serious?!" says Schaffer.

The dinosaurs close in on them, now only feet away. Their sharp claws glisten in the sun's rays and they begin screeching as though communicating with one another. The Baroness takes a few swipes with her sword to warn them off. They back away, but only for a moment. In return the dinosaurs snap at the blade, missing it by inches.

"Whatever the plan is, now might be a good time to do something about it, gentlemen!" says the Baroness with some urgency.

"We need to be going up, not down," replies Burrell, putting a slight dampener on things.

"Speak for yourself!" shouts Vanderbilt. He runs towards the plants with the large leaves.

Following Vanderbilt, seconds later, the group run towards the large-leafed plants. Keeping an eye on the dinosaurs, Burrell and the Baroness keep their weapons drawn and primed. The dinosaurs quickly move towards them.

"Alright, we'll go in twos. Esteban, you go with him. When you get clear enough further down, grab hold of the vines and pull yourselves up. We don't have time to waste – we don't know how long the portal's going to stay open. We've got to get to the higher ground," says Burrell.

"Okay," replies Esteban.

The velociraptors menacingly edge nearer as the Baroness takes a few more swipes, keeping them at bay.

"Okay, are you ready?" Burrell asks them. Vanderbilt, with his bottle in tow, and Esteban, who grabs Magnum under his arm, both reluctantly nod in agreement and start climbing onto and into one of the large leaves. The leaves themselves resemble large cupped water lily leaves, which look sturdy and capable enough of holding their weight.

"Ready?" asks Burrell.

"As we'll ever be!" replies Vanderbilt slightly nervously.

Burrell turns to face the dinosaurs with his cane as the Baroness quickly turns to the leaf, raises her sword and brings it down with force – cutting the leaf clean off from its thick stem.

Vanderbilt and Esteban let out a loud scream as they, along with the leaf, are catapulted into the air! They land on the rocky hill with a thud then hurtle down the hill at speed, holding on for dear life!

The velociraptors look on in agitation and momentary confusion as they watch some of their prey escape on a leaf! The Baroness continues to keep them back with her sword as she lunges and swipes back and forth to deter them. Burrell also does the same with his cane, which, for the most part, is working. In return, the dinosaurs edge ever nearer, snapping more aggressively with anger at the group.

Screechy and Schaffer slowly back away towards the plants as Burrell and the Baroness tighten their formation with their weapons still drawn. The remaining group and the dinosaurs momentarily watch on as the leaf disappears into the mist.

Eleven

HURTLING DOWN THE steep incline, heading into near oblivion, the leaf speeds through the mist. Sitting at the front of the leaf, Vanderbilt struggles to hold onto his bottle as he's continuously hit in the face by the long overhanging vines that appear in batches through the mist. Esteban holds onto Magnum, who looks on frightened at proceedings, his feathers flapping around in the wind.

"We have to jump, sir!" shouts Esteban.

Vanderbilt laughs nervously then smiles, knowing he'll have to jump sooner rather than later. As they both try to get their balance the leaf starts spinning. Both men fall into one another as the leaf continues to build up speed. They pick themselves up, albeit unsteadily, and try to balance themselves as they bump over rocks and undergrowth that makes it difficult for them to stand. Whilst doing so, Esteban stuffs Magnum into his hat.

A cluster of vines become visible at speed through the mist. Vanderbilt prepares to stretch up to reach them. Esteban gets ready to help lift him. Both men time it right. "Now!"

shouts Vanderbilt and lunges high into the air – with Esteban lifting him up. With his bottle in one hand, he grabs a vine for all his worth. Within a split second, he's whooshed off his feet into the air and is swinging back and forth as the leaf carrying Esteban and Magnum continues speeding down the hill into the distance.

Seconds later, Esteban prepares himself to jump and lunges up for the vines. He lets out a yelp and then smiles at having made it. Magnum peeks out from under the hat and sees that they are swinging in mid air. Quickly, he cowers back underneath, using his beak to pull the hat down!

The dinosaurs edge closer and closer towards the remaining group. The Baroness and Burrell swing their sword and cane respectively to try and keep them at bay. The velociraptors occasionally strike against the sword's blade with their sharp claws, trying to knock it out of the Baroness's hand.

With their backs against the large leaves, Schaffer and Screechy begin to whimper slightly at being trapped.

"What are we going to do?!" shouts Screechy.

"The same again!" replies the Baroness.

"Get in, quickly!" shouts Burrell.

As Screechy begins making his way up onto one of the large leaves, one of the dinosaurs, knowing their prey is about to escape again, makes a break for it! The velociraptor quickly bypasses Burrell and the Baroness.

"Look out, Screechy!" shouts Burrell.

"For what?" he asks, oblivious.

He looks up and sees the dinosaur heading straight for

him! He screams at the top of his lungs. The velociraptor responds with a high-pitched screech straight back at him!

Schaffer quickly moves out the way as Screechy runs behind the leaf. The velociraptor looks for Screechy then sees him cowering behind the leaf. It climbs into the leaf as Screechy watches on frozen in fear, then it peers over the edge – and looks Screechy straight in the eye. He begins shaking.

The other two dinosaurs begin to edge towards Schaffer and Screechy. However, Burrell and the Baroness change their formation and create a more aggressive defence.

Screechy makes a run for it as the dinosaur moves to the other end of the leaf.

"Screechy, duck!" shouts the Baroness.

"Where?!"

He looks up and sees the Baroness bringing down her sword with force. The blade cuts through the thick stem of the leaf, slicing it clean off. With the weight of the dinosaur still inside, the leaf falls at speed onto the rocky slope with a thud and speeds down the hill through the mist. Confused at what's happening, the velociraptor wails and screeches as it disappears from view into the mist!

"You saved me, Baroness!" shouts Screechy, trying to cuddle her.

"Never mind that now! Both of you get out of here!" she tells him.

With the other dinosaurs confused, Schaffer and Screechy are able to jump into a large leaf and make good their escape!

"Now!" screams Schaffer.

The Baroness slices their leaf, and they thump onto the rocky hill and speed off through the mist.

Schaffer and Screechy struggle to remain seated in their leaf as it bounces and spins uncontrollably. Ahead of them, breaking through the misty clouds, is the velociraptor on its own leaf. They exchange anxious looks when the dinosaur sees them and screeches violently at the top of its lungs.

The rocky slope makes way for more grass and soil. The cunning velociraptor comes up with a plan and quickly digs its sharp claws into the ground to slow itself down!

Still swinging from the vines, Vanderbilt and Esteban see the leaves heading down towards them – the latter going faster and heading straight for the now slowing dinosaur.

The velociraptor is now nearly stationary, and Schaffer and Screechy are heading straight towards it at speed! Screaming, they crash into the dinosaur. It jumps over them and grabs the rear of their leaf and hangs on with its claws. With the extra weight, the leaf begins spinning and turning even faster.

"Up here!" shouts Vanderbilt at the top of his lungs, his voice echoing through the gorge.

Schaffer and Screechy look up and notice Vanderbilt and Esteban hanging from the vines. As they near them, the dinosaur begins lunging at Schaffer and Screechy, missing them by inches with its razor-sharp claws. It manages to pull itself into the leaf. Both men scream! Screechy quickly digs into his pocket and finds some pistachio nuts. He flings them at the dinosaur, momentarily disorientating it. Schaffer looks sceptically at Screechy, then gives a wry smile at his ingenuity.

The vines that Vanderbilt and Esteban are holding onto appear within striking distance. Schaffer and Screechy ready themselves to jump as the dinosaur focuses on them once more.

"You, up!" Schaffer shouts to Screechy.

"Where …?"

"There!" shouts Schaffer quickly pointing to the approaching vines.

The velociraptor edges nearer, about to pounce …

"Now!" shouts Screechy.

Screechy jumps and Schaffer helps lift him up. He lunges and grabs hold of the vines as the dinosaur takes a swipe at him, missing by inches. Schaffer blows a raspberry towards the dinosaur as he too lunges up and grabs hold of a lower hanging vine, escaping the leaf. Both men now swing free of the dinosaur's clutches. However, the dinosaur has other ideas!

It too jumps from the fast moving leaf and grabs hold of a vine with its sharp teeth and long snout. Schaffer and Screechy scream in panic as the dinosaur swings back and forth only feet from them on the vines! They begin climbing as fast as their panic-stricken, adrenaline-filled bodies will allow. Metres from them, Vanderbilt and Esteban have the same idea and also start hurriedly climbing.

The dinosaur struggles to make any headway and languishes at the bottom of its vine, trying unsuccessfully to climb with its limited use of its short arms and snout.

Twelve

Burrell and the Baroness are pinned in by the dinosaurs that edge ever nearer towards them, sneering and snapping. Their sword and cane are the only things holding them back, but the dinosaurs try their best to knock them out of their hands.

"Well, so much for leading by example! Isn't that the Admiralty way?!" shouts the Baroness.

"I gave that mantle to Vanderbilt, what can I say?" he retorts flippantly.

The Baroness nervously smiles. "Are you ready?" she asks.

"No time like the present! Go for it!"

The Baroness quickly brings out her musket and fires. The dinosaurs flinch and cower at the loud noise whilst the discharged musket ball strikes a large branch of a nearby tree. The branch breaks off and crashes onto the dinosaurs.

Seizing their chance, Burrell and the Baroness run as fast as their legs will carry them. They dive into a leaf, the Baroness using her sword to cut them free. The leaf separates from the stem and catapults them onto the hill. They speed off through the eerie mist.

Annoyed at losing their prey again, the velociraptors shake off the remains of the shattered branch and screech and wail at one another. Seconds later, they jump into a leaf and begin furiously clawing away at the stem. The leaf suddenly rips from the plant and sets off down the hill after Burrell and the Baroness!

Burrell and the Baroness struggle to hold themselves inside the leaf as it bounces and spins down the steep incline. Through the mist, they're sporadically hit by the vines. Burrell briefly manages to make out the others hanging from the vines in the distance, as well as the dinosaur.

"Look!" he shouts to the Baroness, who looks up and sees them. Something catches her eye behind them – the velociraptors on the leaf speeding after them! Given they have a greater weight, they're gaining on their human prey – and rapidly.

"Oh, no!" she shouts.

Burrell notices them too. "This is going to be close!" he shouts.

"Not really what I wanted to hear!" she replies.

"Now I know how pirates feel when I hunt them down!" he replies with a wry smile.

The Baroness lets out a loud, nervous laugh.

"I hope this works!" shouts Burrell. He puts his weight to the left-hand side of the leaf, trying to steer it – it works! The leaf veers, heading towards a large rock.

"What are you doing?!" the Baroness shouts. "Have you lost your mind?!"

"Quite possibly! When we hit the rock – jump!" he responds.

They're only feet below the rest of the group when they hit the rock with force! Both are thrown from the leaf high into the air. They manage to gain great height and grab hold of the vines.

"Wow!" screams the Baroness.

Burrell and the Baroness swing back and forth on the vines due to the force of their impact.

"May I?" asks Burrell, pointing to the Baroness's sword.

She throws him her sword as the velociraptors on the leaf fast approach. The lone dinosaur hanging precariously on the vine screeches at the group.

Burrell times his swing perfectly. He raises the sword and slices the vine on which the dinosaur is hanging. The dinosaur falls straight into the path of the oncoming dinosaurs. It lands with force on top of them, causing the dinosaurs to all fall onto their backs. With their speed now increasing due to the extra weight, they'll have no way of stopping the leaf until it reaches the bottom, giving the group enough time to get away from them.

The leaf disappears into the misty landscape, with the dinosaurs screeches disappearing with it.

"Woo-hoo!" shouts Vanderbilt, "That showed 'em dinosaurs!"

"They've got more tenacity than the King's guards!" says a flippant Baroness.

"Well, you should know! I'm sure you've had your fair share of encounters!" replies Burrell smiling.

The group remain hanging from the vines, albeit with weakening strength, visibly relieved that their pursuers have disappeared.

"Try and get some momentum and swing between the vines over to that rock formation," he tells the group as he points to it.

Some of the group look on confused.

"What, like a monkey, sir?" says Schaffer.

"Exactly, Schaffer!" Burrell replies.

"Well, here goes nothin'!" says Vanderbilt, who begins putting his extra weight to good use. He starts to swing back and forth and gradually builds up enough momentum to bump into Esteban, who in turn begins swinging. Soon enough the whole group are swinging back and forth. As they each build up enough momentum, they jump between vines – almost in unison, like a troop of monkeys.

Despite still being several metres up in the air, they cheer and laugh as they make their way towards the rock formation – relieved that they have made it this far.

Esteban lands first atop the rock, with the others soon following. He lifts his hat up and Magnum slowly peeks out.

"Gone?" the bird sheepishly asks.

"Yes," replies Esteban.

Magnum flies out, flapping his crumpled wings and puffing them up to full bloom. He flies around over the group and checks the area for any unwanted predators.

"All clear!" he tells them.

Meanwhile, Burrell is looking through his telescope towards the higher ground, scouring for the portal. He sees it and smiles – it's still there.

Dusting themselves down, the group head off through jungle with its tall trees and shrubbery towards higher ground. Burrell leads the way with Vanderbilt bringing up the rear.

Thirteen

THE MIST NOW evaporated, the warm midday sun beats down on the lush landscape. Having walked for what feels like hours and sweating in the humidity, the group exit the jungle and come upon an eerily quiet clearing that stretches for miles. It's filled with hundreds of bones – a dinosaur graveyard. Bones of large and small dinosaurs, some of them still in the position in which they died, are as far as the eye can see atop acres of dead grass and vegetation. Frenzied vultures scavenge on a large recently deceased carcass, fighting amongst themselves over its remains.

The group continue walking past, albeit slowly, with an eye on the ever-preying vultures, who notice them but continue to feast on the animal remains instead.

"Look at this place. It's so final. It's like a dinosaurs graveyard," says a slightly solemn Screechy.

"I think that's what it is, Screechy," replies Burrell.

"Well I never... It's like the time when me and the crew had a big turkey on the ship and got down to the bare bones and that... It was 'orrible."

"As horrible as it is, just be thankful you were eating turkey. Many others don't have that privilege," says the Baroness.

"Slightly ironic, is it not, ma'am… pirate, that you, having lived in the biggest palaces in the land before committing treason against the King, should make such a statement?" says Schaffer.

The Baroness turns to Schaffer. "Perhaps, but I didn't always live a privileged lifestyle – far from it," she replies, sounding humble.

"Well, this is great and all, but perhaps we should be focusing on getting ourselves out of here, before *we* become the remains," says Vanderbilt.

"Keep heading over that way. The portal should be over the next ridge," Burrell tells them.

The group continue walking, weary, bedraggled and hungry. Magnum flies with them, keeping a watchful eye out for any unwanted visitors. As they get to the end of the clearing, and the end of the dinosaur graveyard, Burrell takes a long poignant look at it, taking in the sheer scale of history, life and death.

"To think, these animals ruled the world, long ago," he says to himself before joining up with the others.

The group continue walking slowly and wearily, many of them now beginning to become dehydrated. They arrive at the end of a precipice, with a deep gorge between them and the other side. The precipice must be at least several hundred foot deep, darkening into the depths of the earth the further it descends. The gap is too wide to jump.

"Oh no, what are we goin' to do now?" asks a dejected Screechy.

"There's no way across," the Baroness mumbles.

Burrell looks on almost defeated – it was his duty to lead the group to safety and the portal. He scours the area, looking up and down for any narrower gaps or crossings, but there are none.

"We'll have to go down to come back up," says Esteban.

"If we go down into the valley, Esteban... I don't like our chances of making it back up alive," replies Burrell.

Esteban gasps slightly at the statement. Burrell looks over to Magnum, who is clearly tired and hungry, and comes up with a plan.

"Nathaniel, can I borrow your bottle?" he asks Vanderbilt.

Vanderbilt nods in agreement and hands him the bottle. Burrell pours a couple of small drops of rum onto the palm of his hand – just enough to quench Magnum's thirst.

"Magnum, come. Here, drink this. It will give you some strength," says Burrell. "We need you to fly up and down the canyon for us to see if we can cross over anywhere. Can you do that for us?"

Magnum gulps down the little alcohol from Burrell's hand, choking a little. Upon finishing and letting out a light burp, he flaps his wings, then cleans them. His lethargy soon gives way to a more energetic lorikeet as the alcohol kicks in.

"Okay!" he squawks before flying off at speed.

"Good work, and here's me thinking you were going to take a drop yourself," says the Baroness.

"I don't want to deprive Nathaniel of his prized possession, not yet anyway," replies Burrell.

"I heard that!" responds Vanderbilt.

Burrell and the Baroness gently smile at his response.

Screechy, Schaffer and Esteban rest up against some rocks and fallen trees, physically shattered. As they rest and close their eyes, in the distance sound the vultures. A couple of them fly overhead, having finished their feeding frenzy. The group go unobserved as the vultures fly over them and head away.

Burrell decides to take the weight off his feet and sits atop a dead tree trunk. In doing so, he falls straight through it, landing with a thud.

The others laugh at his misfortune and clumsiness, and he joins them. Their laughter is a welcome distraction from their current predicament. However, Burrell studies the trunk more closely and notices that the wood is brittle – dead and bone dry.

"I know that look. You've come up with a plan, haven't you?" asks the Baroness.

Burrell smiles at her. "That I have. If we can find a tree that's long enough to cross the gorge… one that's fallen or dead, then we might be able to use it to cross over to the other side."

"But won't it break like that one?" enquires Schaffer.

"Not if we choose wisely. Make sure it's not brittle. That way it should be strong enough to hold our weight. Some of us more than others …" he says.

Just as Burrell finishes speaking, Magnum returns.

"Nothing!" he squawks.

"That settles it. It's our only option."

The others pick themselves up and begin looking for nearby trees suitable for them to use.

"If we do find a suitable trunk, sir, how on earth are we going to move it?" asks Schaffer.

"Where there's a will, there's a way," he replies, knowing full well he doesn't know how they will overcome the issue.

The majority of the trees and vegetation are lush due to the moisture in the air and the rivers surrounding the gorge. However a few trees that look less healthy catch the attention of the group.

"What about this one?" asks Schaffer.

The leaves are beginning to turn brown. However, Burrell shakes his head, feeling it's not quite dead enough for them to try and tear down. The group continue searching until a trunk catches Burrell's eye.

"This is the one," he tells the group.

A long, not too bulky hollow trunk lies destitute on the ground, surrounded with weeds, rotten leaves and vines. Large gnarly holes are visible throughout the length of the trunk.

Burrell begins unravelling the vines as the others look on curious at his actions. He wraps them around his hands, making sure they are strong and robust.

"May I?" Burrell asks the Baroness, pointing to her sword.

She hands him the sword and he cuts the vines. Bemused, the group watch Burrell as he begins tying the vines through the gnarled holes. He looks up and smiles.

"Trust me."

Fourteen

"ONE, TWO, THREE… heave!" shouts Burrell. Seconds later Burrell, Schaffer and Screechy appear through the undergrowth pulling the tree trunk by the vines draped over their shoulders. Esteban and the Baroness walk either side, also pulling on their respective vines. Vanderbilt has the task of pushing the trunk when the others pull their vines. Collectively they make good headway and stop at the edge of the precipice.

"Now what?" says Vanderbilt.

"Now we keep pushing just enough to balance it over the edge," Burrell replies.

The group go to the back of the trunk and push it with all their might. It slowly scrapes across the rocks and mud as they nudge it over the edge a little at a time until nearly half the trunk is hanging over the gorge. They stop so Burrell can check it.

"If we push anymore it could go over the edge," he says, looking at Esteban and Screechy. "You two are the lightest, so here's the plan. We'll need you two to climb onto the trunk and jump across, then use the vines to help pull it over as we push from this side."

"I'm sorry… you want us to jump onto the trunk – wif that huge drop under us?!" asks a somewhat reluctant Screechy.

"That's correct. If any of us do it, we'll be too heavy and we'll all go over. So we need you and Esteban to cross over first," replies Burrell calmly.

Screechy looks on sceptically, reluctant to oblige.

"I'm not asking as an admiral now, Screechy. I'm asking as a fellow ally, given our situation," he replies.

"I can't, sir. I just can't do it. I… I've got a fear of heights," Screechy says.

"You won't have to look down. Keep your head up and focus on the other side. Esteban will be there to guide you every step of the way," Burrell says, trying to boost Screechy's confidence.

"That's right. I'll be there," interjects Esteban.

Screechy deliberates with himself as the others become slightly impatient. Burrell surreptitiously checks his pocket watch. The Baroness notices this.

"You owe me one," she tells Burrell as she walks to Screechy and puts her arm around his shoulder, clearly trying to take advantage of the fact that he likes her. She talks to him out of ear shot of the others and slowly but surely walks him to the tree trunk. Unbeknownst to him, distracted by their conversation, she helps him onto the tree trunk. Behind her back, she waves quickly for Esteban to join them. The Baroness whispers into Screechy's ear, causing him to smile shyly like a child.

Then, and only then, does he realize that he's atop the tree trunk! He lets out an almighty scream, loud enough to attract any nearby dinosaurs. Esteban quickly jumps onto the trunk to calm him down, then turns to Vanderbilt to signal him to throw him the bottle of rum. He does so. In doing so, the rest of the group quickly sit on the other end of the trunk to provide extra weight and balance to stop the trunk from falling into the gorge.

Esteban catches the bottle and offers Screechy a drink. He duly accepts and takes a gulp to calm his nerves. Esteban takes the bottle off him and gives it back to Vanderbilt.

"That should help calm your nerves. We need you," Esteban tells him.

Screechy calms down and gets his bearings, trying not to look down. Esteban takes hold of the vines and gives some to Screechy to hold and they both slowly, methodically and carefully make their way along the trunk.

Esteban and Screechy reach the end of the trunk, the huge drop beneath them. Screechy momentarily looks down and begins to shake and panic. Esteban holds him steady to stop him falling.

"I'm okay, I'm okay," he tells Esteban. Breathing in and out, Screechy calms himself.

"Are you ready?" Esteban asks.

He nods in agreement.

"Okay. On three. One, two …"

The others watch on with trepidation and anticipation.

"Wait! Wait! Are we jumpin' on free, or free and then jumpin'?!" enquires Screechy just as Esteban is ready to throw himself off the trunk. He pulls himself back from the edge at the last second and, slightly exasperated, nervously shouts, "It's *on* three!"

"Right you are – on free. Are *you* ready?" he asks.

Esteban looks at him for a moment in bemusement, then nods.

"Okay… one, two, free!" shouts Screechy.

Both men take a few big steps and then leap off the end of the trunk almost in slow motion. The others watch on with baited breath. Screechy and Esteban leap through the air and make it safely to the other side, landing on the solid ground opposite. Quickly, they begin pulling the vines and taking the tension as the others jump off the trunk and push it with every muscle they have. It works! The trunk is dragged across, and Screechy and Esteban tie the vines around nearby rocks, securing the trunk in place.

As they sit and catch their breath, Vanderbilt makes his way over successfully, carrying his bottle. Burrell then makes his way over cautiously, trying not to put too much weight onto the trunk as it begins to creak slightly. He makes it across. Schaffer begins making his way across too, just as a flock of pterodactyls fly over them, squawking and screeching. As Schaffer looks up, he loses his balance and slips over the side. He grabs onto one of the trunk's stumps and screams for his life. The Baroness jumps into action as Schaffer's hand begins to slip.

"Grab my hand! Grab it!" she shouts.

Schaffer struggles to grab her outstretched hand as he swings, hanging over the deep gorge.

Esteban and Vanderbilt run towards the trunk, but Burrell stops them.

"No, the trunk won't hold the extra weight," he tells them. "They're on their own."

Magnum too springs into action and grabs the neck of

Schaffer's jacket trying to lift him up, but his weight is too much for Magnum alone to lift.

Schaffer manages to grab the Baroness's hand and she pulls with every ounce of her strength. With Schaffer pushing himself up and Magnum pulling on his neck, the Baroness manages to bring him up. In doing so, however, the integrity of the trunk is compromised. It begins creaking and moving, as though about to give way.

"Pull yourself up, quickly!" the Baroness shouts.

Schaffer gives it everything he has and manages to get himself on top of the trunk. He and Magnum manage to cross over to the other side, but the trunk finally gives way and buckles with the Baroness still on it!

As the trunk disintegrates and falls into the gorge, the Baroness manages to leap and grab hold of a vine that has dislodged itself from the trunk. Thankfully, it's still tied to the rock. She pulls herself up with the help of Schaffer. Sighing heavily with relief, she makes it onto solid ground. The group look shattered after their recent drama.

"Thank you... ma'am," says a grateful and gracious Schaffer to the Baroness as he gives her a hug.

"I don't know about you, but I sure could do with a minute to catch my breath," Vanderbilt says to Burrell.

"For once, Nathaniel, we are in agreement." Burrell too sighs in relief. "Commodore, are you okay?"

Schaffer struggles to breathe, still trying to take it all in. He does, however, nod in agreement.

"Don't forget us poor pirates over here!" the Baroness retorts. She and Screechy lie sprawled out on the ground, exhausted.

Esteban feeds Magnum some pistachio nuts as a reward for his efforts in helping save Schaffer.

Vultures appear overhead as Burrell watches them fly off into the distance. In doing so, he pauses for a moment, contemplating the group's recent events. He looks at them, thankful they are all still alive and well then brings out his pocket watch and checks the time.

Most of the group lie exhausted on the ground, including Schaffer and the Baroness, who continue to take long deep breaths following their drama.

Dinosaur roars can be heard quietly in the distance filling the valleys and air with their malevolent menace.

"We'll take a few more minutes to compose ourselves, then we'll head off," Burrell tells the group.

Fifteen

WITH SLIGHTLY MORE composure and strength about them, the group walk through long grass and colourful plants on a slight incline, heading towards higher ground. Below them in the lower valley, an array of large and small dinosaurs roam freely.

The group momentarily stop as Burrell looks through his telescope towards the peak of the adjacent hill. The portal is still there. However, it's slowly beginning to flicker and lose its strength.

"We need to hurry, I don't think we have much time," Burrell tells the group.

They begin walking again, this time with more urgency and purpose. Burrell leads them through the long grass. Quiet squawks and screeches sound – and gradually begin to get louder. The group look around but can't see anything over the long grass.

Magnum flies above them, also looking around, but can't see anything. Suddenly, behind them the grass begins to move, as though something large is moving fast towards them.

"Run!" squawks Magnum at the top of his lungs.

Panicked, the group run as fast as they can.

Behind them, flying through the undergrowth at speed, are two pterodactyls!

Esteban's eyes light up in horror as he brings up the rear of the group – directly in the firing line! At the last second he dives out of their way. They miss him by inches.

The flying dinosaurs now set their focus on the others. Burrell and the Baroness arm themselves with their cane and sword. Vanderbilt manages to strike one with his bottle, forcing it up and out of danger for the time being. In doing so, though, he causes the pterodactyls to screech and squawk even louder, which will inevitably bring more danger to the group.

One of the pterodactyls makes for Burrell and the Baroness.

"Move!" shouts Burrell to the others, who pick themselves up and run flat out towards the flickering portal.

The Baroness grabs her musket and fires. The musket ball misses the large predators by inches. However, the loud bang momentarily frightens them off and they back away from the group.

Exiting the long undergrowth, the group have a clear run to the portal, which is getting dimmer.

From behind them in the distance sounds a large roar! Frightened, the group look around and see the huge T-rex from earlier making its way towards them at speed through the adjacent undergrowth and trees, almost galloping towards them!

"Oh no, this is not good!" shouts Burrell.

The group continue running up the hill, Burrell and the Baroness now bringing up the rear. The T-rex makes ground on them quickly as its loud, threatening roar booms once again from its large jaws, engulfing the hillside in its booming call.

"Hurry, head for the top!" shouts Burrell to the others.

"Easy for you to say, you're not carrying extra weight around your belly like some of us!" replies Vanderbilt.

The T-rex suddenly appears, smashing its way through some small trees behind them. It chases them, closing in quickly.

"Hurry!" shouts Schaffer.

As the group near the top, the two pterodactyls reappear – aiming straight for the group! The T-rex gains on them as they run flat out up the grassy hill towards the ever weakening portal.

"Esteban, we need to do the fire trick!" says Vanderbilt.

"Good idea!" replies Esteban. "Throw me your sword and casing Baroness!" he shouts.

Slightly sceptical at his motives, but with nothing to lose, the Baroness flings him her sword. Esteban takes the sword out of its metal casing – and purposely lets go of Magnum, who he had been carrying.

The deadly T-rex gains on them. Vanderbilt suddenly stops and lifts up his bottle preparing to take a drink!

"I hardly think this is the time, Nathaniel!" shouts Burrell, noticing Vanderbilt with his rum.

"On the contrary… You're not the only man with a plan around here ya' know!" shouts Vanderbilt as he takes a massive drink of his overproof rum.

Burrell looks quizzical as Esteban stops running too. Vanderbilt turns around and spits his rum out with gusto! As he does so, Esteban forcibly bangs together the sword and its metal casing – causing a spark!

Suddenly the overproof rum ignites in a ball of fire! The T-rex roars in fear and quickly stops in its tracks, scared. Magnum squawks loudly, cowering away from the flames.

"Go away!" Magnum squawks to the T-rex.

The T-rex runs away down the hill frightened. Burrell, who's slowed down his pace looks to Vanderbilt – and doffs his hat to him. Vanderbilt and Esteban start running again and try to catch up with the others. Esteban flings the Baroness back her sword and casing.

The pterodactyls are also momentarily frightened by the fireball and deviate from their course.

"A little party trick I learnt in my youth!" shouts Vanderbilt to Burrell.

"You're quite a rambunctious soul!" shouts Burrell to Vanderbilt. "I may have underestimated you, Nathaniel!"

"That you did, Wesley, but we can discuss that later, once you get me some more rum!" he replies.

"Why didn't you do that earlier in the cave to create the fire?" asks the Baroness.

"I didn't want to waste any rum!" retorts Vanderbilt.

"Well, we couldn't have that now!" replies the Baroness sarcastically.

The group reach the top after their run-in with the T-rex as the pterodactyls fly over them, screeching and squawking loudly.

The portal slowly begins to glisten and change colour, getting ever weaker in strength. Noticing this, Burrell shouts to the others, "Come on – hurry up!"

The pterodactyls swoop down. One grabs Burrell and the other grabs Esteban, and they are picked up off the ground! Burrell quickly uses his cane and starts swinging and swiping at the pterodactyl. The large flying dinosaur puts up a little fight but ultimately let's him go. He falls onto the rocky ridge.

Esteban starts pushing and hitting his abductor, to no

avail. Magnum suddenly appears in front of the pterodactyl and starts pecking at its eyes. The dinosaur quickly becomes disorientated and flies downwards, causing Esteban to fall. He lands on the ridge safely and the Baroness helps pick him up.

They continue to the portal – which is still glistening and changing colours. The Baroness swings her sword and casing back and forth to fend off one of the returning pterodactyls.

The glistening colours of the portal suddenly catch the attention of one of the pterodactyls. It flies towards it, distracted by the bright lights and almost kaleidoscopic colours and causing it to crash into the rocks, some of which fall and crumble onto the ridge.

"How are we going to get up now?!" shouts Screechy.

The rocks were the only way the group could reach the portal.

"Make a human ladder!" replies Burrell.

"Good idea!" says the Baroness.

"I'll distract them," squawks Magnum to Burrell.

"Thanks, Magnum," he replies.

"Quickly, hurry," the Baroness tells the others.

Magnum flies towards the pterodactyls, trying to draw their attention and distract them away from the group. He flies around in circles, and up and down. The pterodactyls follow in hot pursuit – snapping at Magnum's wings.

The group start to create a human ladder, with Vanderbilt at the base, then Schaffer on his shoulders – albeit slightly unsteady. Vanderbilt sways back and forth, trying to get his balance right, as Schaffer grips tightly onto his head. He steadies himself, and Esteban and Screechy climb on top of Schaffer. The Baroness then quickly climbs up. Screechy smiles, just about to push her bum.

"Don't even think about it, Screechy!" she tells him.

She reaches the higher rocks, then pulls Screechy up, then Esteban, who in turn helps up Schaffer and Vanderbilt.

"Come on, Admiral!" shouts Schaffer.

"I'll be right with you!" shouts Burrell, as he takes a long run, extends his cane – using it like a pole vault – and makes a huge leap towards the group! He manages to get a foothold on the rocks and is pulled up by the others.

"Thanks," he says to the group. He turns to Magnum and shouts, "Magnum, come on!"

Magnum makes his way towards the group, as do the pterodactyls! The portal begins to emit a high-pitched noise as it shines brighter and changes colour. At the same time, it begins to get smaller, weaker and more transparent against the rocky backdrop.

"Let's see if we can get home!" shouts Burrell.

"Are you sure about this, sir?" asks Schaffer.

"What other choice do we 'ave?" says Screechy.

"Well, that was certainly quite an adventure, Admirals!" shouts the Baroness.

"I'm always up for an adventure or two – with or without pirates," replies Vanderbilt playfully.

"Well, let's see if we can take these Admiralty Adventures home, shall we!?" shouts Burrell.

The portal continues to make high-pitched sounds. The group join hands and Vanderbilt leads the group into the portal. One by one, they begin to vanish. Magnum flies towards them and squeezes under Esteban's hat, as he goes into the portal and vanishes. Before leaving the Jurassic period behind, Burrell takes one last look before he too vanishes into the portal, with only moments to spare.

Seconds later, the portal closes up and disappears! The pterodactyls aim for them – but they've all gone. At speed, they crash into the remaining rocks, smashing them to bits.

The group fly through the multicoloured wormhole vortex, spinning and flipping. They scream as a bright light appears. In the blink of an eye, they all vanish. Perhaps they've finally made it back home …

About the Author

With a passion for writing, and having been brought up on movies, stories and adventure, C.E. Cumming decided to pen his debut book "The Admiralty Adventures – Treasure of the High Seas" based upon one of the many short scripts he'd written.

Having worked on movie sets, and having written hundreds of stories and ideas over the years, the time had come for him to take the leap of faith into the publishing world and enact the well known proverb: nothing ventured, nothing gained!

Residing in Scotland, he spends his time writing screenplays, freelance writing, watching movies and running a small creative media company. As his passion for creating continues to flourish, his imagination continues to conjure up ever more magic.

The Admiralty Adventures – Treasure of the High Seas is his first published work.

Printed in Poland
by Amazon Fulfillment
Poland Sp. z o.o., Wrocław